Don Camillo and Company

The first completely new Don Camillo since the 1960s, these stories are a collector's item. It is suspected, after a close study of how the original English publisher edited some of its translations in the 1950s and '60s, that many stories in the canon were overlooked on account of their being, in the publisher's opinion, too overtly political, or violent, or irreverent for the palate of their readers. Even if the publisher's judgements felt justified then, times have moved on and there is certainly nothing to upset anybody in this treasure trove of priceless parables minted from life in La Bassa, the so-called Lower Plain between the Po River and the Apennine mountains in northern Italy, which is the author's inspiration. These tales are novel enchantments for those who already know Don Camillo, and a very special entré to his world for those who don't.

Giovannino Guareschi, known as Giovanni to his millions of readers, was born at Fontanelle in the Valley of the Po on May Day, 1908. He found his vocation when he sent some cartoons he had drawn to the satirical magazine, *Il Bartoldo*. Later he founded his own magazine, *Candido*, and between 1946 and 1966 he wrote over 300 stories featuring Don Camillo, a character who has done for Italy what Cervantes' Don Quixote did for Spain. Beloved all over the world by readers from 10 to 100, Don Camillo has been feted not only in books but in films, in series on TV, on radio and most recently in audiobook form.

Some Reviews

'Inimitable, delicious, full of pure fun' *The Observer*

'Charming and enchanting … witty and wise' *Edinburgh Evening News*

'Written with such warmth and simplicity, so concerned with the trivialities of everyday life and giving us so shrewd a glimpse into the minds of the people …' *London Evening News*

'You'll find Don Camillo not just enchanting and lovable, and at times hilariously funny, but also strangely moving in his simple but certain faith.' *BBC Radio – 'Books by the Fire'*

DON CAMILLO AND COMPANY

GIOVANNI GUARESCHI

PILOT PRODUCTIONS

Published by Pilot Productions in 2018
Grove Farm Sawdon, North Yorkshire YO13 9DY

A catalogue record for this book is available
from the British Library

ISBN 978-1-900064-40-8

Jacket design by BerniStevensdesign.com

Typeset in Galliard by Mark Heslington Ltd,
Scarborough, North Yorkshire YO11 3PU

Contents

Editor's Preface – the Background

*D*ON CAMILLO AND COMPANY brings us once more to
the lowland plain of Emilia-Romagna, between the
River Po to the north and the Apennines to the south,
where Giovanni Guareschi was born and where he set
most of his inimitable stories about Don Camillo and
Peppone. *La Bassa*, as it is known, was always 'a little
world apart'. It lies but a short distance from the city of
Parma, but is a million miles from any city in spirit.

Francesco Luigi Campari gave us to believe it is Nature's
paradise.[1] Campari wrote of the fecundity of the soil
beneath a sky of 'beautiful azure-blue'. Looking over the
broad sandbanks of the Po he saw 'not one single palm
less than luxuriantly green'; his picture was of 'fields of
waving corn, all bordered by rows of vines, punctuated at
intervals with small field-maples and crowned with banks
of mature mulberry trees . . . thick clumps of willow
bristling on the river banks . . . broad rich stands of
poplar, interspersed here and there with alders and osiers
or prettily adorned with perfumed honeysuckles, which
embrace them and form arbours and steeples, sprinkled
with tiny coloured bells.'

And then the wildlife: 'no small quantity of hare, and
from time to time the air is cloven by quails, turtle doves,
partridges with grizzled plumage, woodcocks that peck
the earth into a sieve, and other birds of step. Overhead,
great flocks of fleet starlings and in winter schools of
duck pattern the sky across the Po, and the alert white
gull, gleaming watchful on the wing, swoops and grabs
for fish.' While 'riverside, the reeds conceal the many-
coloured kingfisher, reed warbler, water-loving moorhen
and crafty coot. You can hear the curlew's distinctive cry

---

[1] *Un castello del parmigiano attraverso i secoli* by Luigi Campari (1910).

and spot herons, plovers, lapwings and other waterfowl, rapacious falcons and circling buzzards (terror of brooding hens), possibly at night even the barn owl and silent nightjar . . .'

It sounds like paradise indeed, and so it is still today. And this is why, as Guareschi attests, 'Things can happen here which don't happen anywhere else, things which are always in tune with the landscape. And the air you breathe there is special, inspiring both the living and the dead; and even the dogs have souls.'

What Guareschi did was to add character to this picture of the region, the character of his people, a hard, rural, agricultural people whose preoccupations were largely associated with the land.

He was imbued with the spirit of the place and knew the people inside out because he was one of them. 'This is the Lower Plain,' he wrote, 'a land where there are people who don't baptise their children, and where blasphemy is not to deny God, but to spite God . . . And where the passion for politics is so intense that it becomes worrying.'

'Worrying' because the political climate of La Bassa was extreme. The fascist dictator Benito Mussolini was born here, his blackshirts rampant; then after Il Duce's execution by the people in 1945, the region saw the greatest concentration of Soviet communism anywhere in Italy.

Emerging from his experience as a prisoner-of-war of the Nazis, where he kept his comrades' spirits high, Guareschi was clear in his mind that totalitarianism – any form of dictatorial government that polices people's minds – is susceptible in particular to humour. With humour his weapon – satirical, absurdist, sometimes even slapstick – he set out to puncture the totalitarian balloon.

Guareschi launched the first of the Don Camillo

stories in his satirical magazine *Candido* in 1946, and following the fall of the Italian monarchy that same year, the magazine went on to play a pivotal role in the defeat of the Communists in the general election of the first Republican Parliament two years later.

Guareschi's humour not only raised his people's spirits and reminded them how to laugh, it triggered their capacity to think for themselves, a capacity which comes from within. In 'Comrade Penèlopo' Don Camillo says to Peppone, 'I don't yearn for the sort of freedom you go on about,' because being a communist the mayor is not free to follow his own conscience, his 'inner voice'. This is the ultimate prison for Don Camillo, the key to the prison door the voice of his conscience personified by Christ on the cross above the High Altar, for whom blessedly, as Guareschi writes in 'The Travelling Comrade', politics are a mystery.

Guareschi advises us to follow our conscience rather than any political dogma. In conversation with the God within, the priest Don Camillo's personal politics and prejudices are exposed and, with fascinating insights and gentle humour, paths of action are suggested which, with the benefit of hindsight, we come to see make things right.

Convinced of his people's 'high sense of humour' and underlying generous disposition, Guareschi felt sure that once they engaged in a similar dialogue with their inner voice, the outcome would be no different. Certainly this is borne out by Peppone, whose true character time and again emerges as distinct from the oppressive ideology which, as communist mayor, he serves. And it is then that he and Don Camillo can work together to the benefit of the people.

Guareschi's approach was more subtle and enlightened than the Vatican's at the time. Pope Pius XII's Decree

Against Communism in 1949 excommunicated Catholics who professed the Soviet ideology. More politics, more conflict. 'The priests want to turn local Catholics against us, so they've excommunicated us and banned us from entering the church,' says Peppone in 'L'Étranger'.

The stories in *Don Camillo and Company* were written between 1947 and 1963 and the date of each is given in the Contents list. Not all are contemporaneous with their writing, some look back into the pre-war past, while others reverberate with the huge changes that the 1950s and 1960s brought to Italy and find footholds universally in a yet more modern world.

In 'The Little Curate', Don Camillo's assistant paints the face and hands of one of the angels in the Christmas nativity scene black. Don Camillo objects. The curate leaves us with the suggestion that Don Camillo might be guilty of being racist. There is dialogue concerning 'the facts' of the history of the nativity and of the science of colour and so on, and before we know it the politics of the scenario have overtaken the celebration of the nativity of Christ, and threatened to paint the traditionalist Don Camillo's soul black. On this occasion Guareschi does not bring the voice of Don Camillo's conscience into play. The priest scrubs the angel clean, goes to bed and sleeps soundly.

We may suppose that Don Camillo is going to struggle with some of the changes that are afoot in the world, especially if he goes to bed without signing off with *il Cristo* first. But there is more than a hint of another, more subtle theme being unveiled here, an observation about political correctness (a phrase not yet in common usage) and the oppressive politicising of life in the modern world, which seeks to sanitise our thinking not unlike the dictator politics of totalitarianism.

In 1962–3 Guareschi was invited to make a documentary

with the film maker Pier Paolo Pasolini called *La Rabbia* (*Rage*). They were to take half the film each to address society's ills in this era of great intellectual ferment and transition, and to pit their views against one another. In the event Guareschi had much to say in agreement with Pasolini. For example, both were opposed to modernity – to the materialism of the modern world, to consumerism and to the Americanisation of Italy. But notably Pasolini's approach, which is powerfully channelled Marxist diatribe, does not have the lightness of touch of Guareschi's. With humour as his weapon Guareschi juxtaposes the serious with the satirical, which deepens the appeal of his argument.

As Marxist, Pasolini identifies the only 'true' and free class of people as those as yet untainted by bourgeois values – he fights for the disaffected sub-proletariat to prevent it being sucked into the lower middle-class; he fights for the African tribesman against imperial exploitation with all the passion of a Rousseau, whose myth of the *bon sauvage* idealised tribal man living in a state of Nature. For Pasolini the tribesman can do no wrong, so cruelly has the white man exploited him throughout history. Guareschi provoked Pasolini about this. He says: 'When I see a black man cutting a white man's throat, I say "poor white man"; you say, "poor black man".'

For Pasolini, the rhythms of tribal dance point to a pure, innocent natural way of life of which the decadent, bourgeois white man is ignorant. Guareschi uses music ironically to question this heavily loaded political statement, attaching a sound track of a military march to footage of black warriors performing a frenetic tribal dance. It is an extraordinary moment in the film, for the rhythms of the white man's music fit the black man's dance so perfectly that we cannot believe that they are not meant for one another.

It was a great disappointment to Guareschi that the films of the Don Camillo stories, made between 1952 and 1965, for all their commercial success, failed to grasp his deeper purpose. But the greater tragedy of Guareschi's life is that his mission led to actual imprisonment, following cases against him brought by Italy's President Luigi Einaudi (over a cartoon depicting him surrounded by a presidential guard of giant bottles of Nebbiolo wine), and by Alcide De Gasperi after Guareschi published photocopies of two wartime letters from the former Prime Minister asking the Allies to bomb the outskirts of Rome in order to demoralise German collaborators.

Thirteen months in prison were followed by six months' probation at home. Conditions in jail were atrocious; he suffered worse, he said, than he did in the Nazi prison camps. He lost weight, his cell was one of the coldest; in winter the temperature reached minus twenty degrees. After 400 days, Giovanni said: 'I don't hate anyone, but I didn't imagine that Italians could be so aggressive against a simple journalist. The SS who were carrying out surveillance on me during my time in the lagers were angels in comparison.'

By 1956, on account of this experience, Giovanni's health had deteriorated and he began to spend time in Switzerland, in 1959 making a second home at Cademario, a village in the district of Lugano in the Swiss canton of Ticino. He died on the 22nd of July, 1968, in Cervia on the east coast of Italy, aged 60.

The feeling in Italy was that the authorities had, throughout his life, treated him shabbily. The word was that Don Camillo had done for Italy what Cervantes' Don Quixote did for Spain, and might be described similarly as 'the genius of the Italian nation'.

Piers Dudgeon, May 2018

Introduction by Giovanni Guareschi

I AM PERPETUALLY irritated by the virtue of the punctilious pen pushers who have penetrated the most unsuspected places and lie in ambush wherever I go. They favour me with a bored and pitying glance when I rush in at the last minute before the deadline with my typewritten pages and India-ink drawings, 'Poor, Guareschi! Just under the rope, as usual!' they are obviously thinking.

At such times I am full of coffee, nicotine, bicarbonate of soda, and fatigue. My clothes are sticking to me because I haven't taken them off for three days; I have dirty hands and stubble on my chin. My mouth is furry and my head, stomach, heart, and liver are all aching. A lock of unkempt hair is hanging down over my nose and black dots dance before my eyes.

'Why do you always wait until the very last minute?' they ask me. 'Why don't you do your work little by little, while there is still plenty of time?'

But if I had paid attention to the punctilious pen pushers, I wouldn't have got even as far as I am today.

I remember distinctly the day of 23 December 1946. Because of Christmas, the work had to be in 'ahead of time', as the pen pushers put it. At that time, besides editing the magazine *Candido*, I wrote stories for *Oggi*, another weekly put out by the same publisher. On 23 December, then, I was up to my ears in trouble. When evening came I had done my piece for *Oggi* and it had been set up by the printer, but the last page of *Candido* was still unfinished.

'Closing up *Candido*!' shouted the copy boy.

What was I to do? I lifted the piece out of *Oggi*, had it reset in larger type and put it into my own paper.

'God's will be done!' I exclaimed.

And then, since there was another half hour before the deadline of *Oggi*, I wrote a hasty story to fill the gap.

'God's will be done!' I said again.

And God must have willed exactly what proceeded to happen. For God is no punctilious pen pusher. Because, if I had heeded all the good advice poured into my ear, Don Camillo, Peppone and all the other characters in this book would have perished on the day they were born, that 23 December 1946. For the very first story of the series was written for *Oggi*, and if it had appeared there, it would have gone the way of its predecessors, and no one would have heard of it again.

But after it came out in *Candido*, I received so many letters from my two dozen subscribers that I wrote a second story about the big priest and the big Red mayor of a village in the Po River valley. Now, what with one joke following after another, I turned in three hours late, to the disgust of the punctilious pen pushers – the two hundredth instalment of the adventures of Don Camillo. And an hour later a letter arrived from France to announce the sale of eight hundred thousand copies of my first published volume,

And so I am not in the least bit sorry to have put off until the morrow that which I could perfectly well have done the day or the month before. At times it saddens me to look over the things I have written, but I don't suffer too awfully much because I can honestly say that I did my best not to write them. And I outdid myself in putting them off from day to day.

There, my friends, is the story of how the priest and the mayor of a village in the Po River valley were born. Two hundred times I have pulled the strings and made them do the most extravagant things that anyone can imagine. So extravagant that often they are literally true. Over and over I complain: 'Now that I've brought them into the world, what shall I do about them? Kill them off and call it a day?'

It is not that I claim to be their 'creator'; all I did was put words into their mouths. The river country of The Little World created them; I crossed their path, linked their arms with mine and made them run through the alphabet, from one end to another. In the last weeks of 1951, when the mighty river overran its banks and flooded the fields of the happy valley, readers from other countries sent me blankets and parcels of clothing marked 'For the people of Don Camillo and Peppone'. Then, briefly, I imagined that instead of being an unimportant fool I was an important one.

I gave all due explanation of the river valley and its little world in the preface to the first volume, and today I can subscribe to every word I said there. I don't know what will be the fate of this book of stories and I refuse to worry about it. I know that when I was a little boy I used to sit on the bank of the mighty river and say to myself: 'Who knows? Perhaps when I'm grown up I'll manage to get to the other side.'

My greatest dream was to own a bicycle. Now I am forty-six years old and the bicycle is mine. Often I go to sit on the river bank where I sat as a boy. And as I chew a blade of grass I can't help thinking: 'After all, this side is the better.' I listen to the stories borne down the mighty river, and people say: 'He grows more absurd every year!'

Which isn't true, because I was absurd from the very beginning. Thanks be to God.

'This is how they told it to me.'

Il Biondo

BRUSCO ARRIVED AT the Presbytery, highly embarrassed: 'Biondo has sent his brother to say he doesn't want you to attend him at his bedside or at his funeral.'

Don Camillo leaped to his feet, his fists clenched, then relaxed and sat down again.

'I'm sorry to hear that,' he said to Brusco. 'I'll ask the priest at Castelletto to attend him instead.'

Brusco shook his head and explained. 'No, Biondo's got nothing against you. He just doesn't want a priest. Not even the Bishop himself. He's made his brother swear that if he sees a priest near the house he'll shoot him.'

It was the first time anything like this had happened in the village, and Don Camillo tried to explain to Brusco the enormity of what was at stake, but Brusco threw out his arms.

'That's democracy,' he said. 'Everyone may choose to die the way they want.'

Before consulting the crucified Christ above the high altar, Don Camillo spent a long time walking up and down, trying to work up the courage. In the end, he spoke with a weary despair.

'I don't understand,' he concluded. 'I baptised Biondo, he took his first Communion here, he always paid attention at Sunday school. Until a couple of years ago he was in church every Sunday. And now he comes up with this heresy! . . . My conscience is troubling me.'

'Why is *your* conscience troubling you, Don Camillo? What does Biondo's decision have to do with you?' asked Jesus.

'I'm afraid it may be because of . . . a post,' whispered Don Camillo.

'A post?'

'Well, you see, a couple of months ago I found Biondo pinning propaganda sheets on the church wall, and there happened to be a stout stake nearby, and so the stake ended up getting broken on his back. . . It was an old stake, completely worm-eaten. . .'

Jesus did not respond.

'I wouldn't want that to be the reason for this hatred of priests and religion. . .' Don Camillo continued.

'It is . . . possible,' replied Jesus. And since he added no further explanation, Don Camillo shut himself away in the presbytery with a volcano erupting in his brain.

Late that evening a small woman arrived, all wrapped up in a cloak. It turned out to be Biondo's sister.

'Don Camillo,' she stammered, 'In the name of God, come and see him. He's dying!'

'How can I?' replied Don Camillo. 'How can I come if he doesn't want me?'

'No, it's not him,' the little woman exclaimed, 'it's our brother. If he knew I'd come to you he'd kill me.'

'Let's go,' cried Don Camillo.

The woman put her hands over her face.

'But what if he sees you?' she sobbed. 'He'll shoot you if he sees you. And if he doesn't shoot you, he'll shoot me instead. We must make sure he doesn't know it's you.'

Don Camillo put on a big cloak and hurtled across the fields followed by the woman. After half an hour they arrived at Cabianca, which was an isolated farm building. They stopped at the hedge by the vegetable garden.

'I'll go in by the kitchen door,' murmured the woman. 'If it's all clear I'll signal to you with the lamp.'

The woman disappeared silently into the night and, shortly afterwards, a light moved at a ground floor window. Don Camillo took off his shoes so he'd make no noise, and was immediately in the kitchen. Fortunately the sick man was in the next room, while his brother was asleep on the first floor.

Biondo's eyes were open and he sighed as soon as he saw Don Camillo.

'Did you call me?' asked Don Camillo.

'Yes.'

Don Camillo bolted the door and went to kneel by the bed so that Biondo could whisper in his ear. He didn't have much to say, but when he stood up again, Don Camillo was sweating. And not from the heat, because the room was freezing. He knelt down again and spoke for a long time in Biondo's ear, and Biondo listened with staring eyes and nodded to show he agreed.

'Don Camillo,' he whispered at the end, 'don't abandon me on the road. I want you to accompany me to the cemetery. Swear it.'

'. . . I swear.'

In the garden, Don Camillo found the woman and told her that Biondo wanted him to accompany the coffin to the cemetery, and Biondo's sister fell into despair. That way his brother would discover everything and would murder her! She was half mad with fear.

'Keep calm,' Don Camillo reassured her.

When Don Camillo returned to the church, he knelt before Christ and spoke at length on Biondo's behalf.

Christ was so swamped by the torrent of words that he felt compelled to promise him –

'I will do everything possible, Don Camillo.'

The next morning word came that Biondo was dead, and so Don Camillo was kept busy all that day and then, late in the evening, he went to present himself before Christ.

'Jesus,' he said, 'I need special permission.'

'What do you mean?'

'A free hand for three hours. And I agree that if I make a mess of things during these three hours, I'll pay for it.'

In the dead man's room they had dismantled his bed and set up two trestles in its place, on which stood an open coffin covered with the red flag. At each corner there was a candle. On a chair, with his face in his hands, was Peppone, who had been keeping vigil by the corpse.

A noise made him lift his head and he found himself suddenly confronted by a stranger with a big hat over his eyes and a handkerchief over his mouth. As he was brandishing a machine gun, Peppone stood up and put up his hands.

'Take that coffin and carry it outside,' the stranger ordered. Peppone was as strong as an elephant, and of course fear doubles your strength. He carried the coffin into the garden and put it on a cart, but first he had to take another coffin of the same kind off the cart, and the stranger helped him to put Biondo's on the trestles in place of the first one.

'Now forget what you've seen, if you value your hide,' the stranger warned him.

Ten minutes later, the stranger slipped away, driving Biondo's coffin on the cart into open country. When he stopped, he removed the handkerchief from his face and the big hat from his head and started slowly pulling the cart, chanting softly . . .

The old sexton was standing by the little gate of the cemetery.

'All well, Don Camillo?'

'All well.'

They carried the coffin into the small cemetery chapel.

'Tomorrow night I will take away the coffin that they'll bring here tomorrow and put this one in its place. Leave it to me, Don Camillo.'

The funeral was held with a great show of flags and music, and at midday Peppone made his way to the presbytery.

'What was the point of you clowning around like that?' said Peppone to Don Camillo. 'I scarcely recognised you.'

'I had to play out the comic charade,' said Don Camillo. 'I'd sworn to Biondo that I would accompany him to the cemetery. Biondo's sister called on me to come to him at the end. But Biondo's brother didn't want me anywhere near him. You know what he is like.'

'And why didn't he want you to see Biondo?'

'Who knows?' exclaimed Don Camillo.

And he was careful not to tell him that he knew perfectly well why the brother hadn't wanted Biondo to see a priest at the end: out of fear that he would confess that, *temporibus illis*, the two of them had done away with the young man from Castellina.[2] As Don Camillo now knew, it was Biondo's brother who had done the whole thing; Biondo himself had just been the lookout.

---

[2] The man whose murder is the focus of 'Nocturne with Bells' in *The Little World of Don Camillo*, possibly itself an oblique reference to the story of the seven Cervi brothers, legendary partisans executed by the Nazis – see https://bit.ly/1v39Y00. The Cervi brothers led the local peasant resistance to Benito Mussolini, retreating to the mountains near Reggio and setting up partisan units to fight his fascist forces and their German backers.

'Only *you* know if you did well or not,' muttered Peppone. 'I was also sorry to think that boy would not die in the grace of God ... So, tell me, Don Camillo: what did you put in the coffin we carried to the cemetery?'

'Straw,' the priest answered.

'Straw? And besides the straw?'

'That plaster thing that stood on the column in the middle of the piazza until last week.'

'Ah!' roared Peppone. 'The bust of Lenin! So it was *you* who stole it!'[3]

'Yes, and you'd better keep quiet about that, because if it gets out that you and your comrades have buried Vladimir Lenin himself, the whole world will laugh at you.'

'I'll laugh when they bury *you*!' shouted Peppone as he went on his way.

---

[3] The legendary bust of Lenin was cast in bronze in 1922 in Lugansk (Ukraine), but it disappeared during the Nazi occupation of the Soviet city twenty years later and mysteriously found its way to Italy. No one knows how. After the end of the war, the bust was returned to the Soviet Union, but in 1970 an official gift of it was made to Cavriago in the province of Reggio Emilia (the Stalingrad of Italy, a town 30 miles or so south-east of Guareschi's birthplace, Fontanelle) – because Lenin himself expressly cited Cavriago in one of his speeches, praising the town for its application of socialism. Today the original bust is still on display in the Cultural Centre of Cavriago, and a copy occupies pride of place in the town square (Piazza Lenin). It is one of the very rare monuments to Lenin that survive in modern times.

Victim of Depreciation

THE LANDLORD OF the Mill Inn opened up at eight, and by ten past the hour he already had a customer: a big chap aged about forty-five, down at heel and with strange eyes. The landlord had never seen such a face before: it had to have come from far away.

The man ate half a basket of bread, some salami, cheese, and eggs. Swollen up like a toad, he then proceeded to pull a 1,000-lire note out of his pocket.

'Bring me a glass of cognac and settle up with this,' he said.

The landlord could see straight away that the note was good. Off he went and came back with the glass and the change. The big man looked puzzled at the money returned to him, and counted it.

'You've given me 410 lire,' he said. 'I gave you a thousand.'

The landlord of the Mill was a brisk sort of fellow and at once he took a slate from a nearby table and starting writing on it with a piece of chalk.

'Bread 100, salami 250, eggs 100, cheese 100, and 40 lire for the cognac. Total 590. From 1,000 leaves 410. You get the picture?'

The big man looked at his change, then at the slate, then at the landlord.

'I don't understand,' he stammered. '. . . What I ate comes to 590 lire?'

'If you go somewhere else, you'll eat worse and spend 650,' replied the landlord. 'Try it: you'll see.'

A woman came in to buy a piece of cheese, a flask of oil and a box of matches, for the Mill was not just a pub but offered skittles and home-cooking, groceries and a range of items stocked exclusively. The big man saw she too was paying with a 1,000-lire note, and without a word of complaint went away with 320 lire change.

'Life *is* expensive,' sighed the landlord, coming back to the big man's table. 'Nowadays, when evening comes, you can fool yourself that you've got a till full of money. But then all you have to do is think that just to buy a clapped-out old bike like that one there, you need to fork out 35,000 lire, and it makes you want to weep.'

The big man put his change in his pocket. He didn't even drink his cognac. He stood up, touched his hat and marched out, hesitating only to look in the shoemaker's window, and then the men's outfitters, whereupon, after reading the price tags on what was for sale, he felt his forehead break out in a sweat. Turning into the first alleyway he came to, he walked briskly as if someone was after him, only stopping when he was in open country.

He felt like crying, yelling, smashing people's faces in, bashing his head against the wall. Then he was overcome with melancholy, sat down on a tree stump, dug a packet out of his sack and opened it. It was a block of 1,000-lire notes. He counted them slowly and there were forty-nine. He thought again about the 590 lire at the pub, and about the price tags on the clothes and shoes.

*

He had arrived at nightfall from another world, as if suddenly woken from a long sleep. He had walked through the fields, arrested every now and then by the distant barking of a dog or the smell of wet earth.

The night was black as ink and, once in sight of the first lights of the little town, he'd had difficulty getting his bearings. Then, recognising the Molinetto dyke, he walked towards the Rossi thicket, his heart pounding with anxiety because he didn't know if the Church by the Bridge would still be there. They could have pulled it down after all this time: it had been a ruin even then, and no good for anything. If they *had* knocked it down, well, that would be that.

But when he came around the bend, there it was, fifty metres ahead of him, exactly as he'd remembered it.

He'd walked all the way round the solitary and long abandoned little church, and entered through the little window at the back. Once inside, his heart had started pounding again: supposing the roof had fallen in? He summoned the courage to look up. Luckily the roof was there: God was still protecting him. He climbed the steps to the organ loft and then up into the vault above the altar. But now his strength ebbed away; he threw himself down onto the floor of the vault and fell straightway to sleep.

He awakened at six in the morning, with the sky already light. The great master beam of oak was still there, black and intact, two metres above his head. By scraping the skin of his hands he managed to get a hold on it and, hanging there from the wood of the roof, he became like an enormous, monstrous bat and began to feel around the upper side of the beam, and then there was the hole, and inside the hole the tube of zinc.

Once down, he opened the tube, and wrapped in the thick oily paper, neat and intact, his 1,000-lire notes. He had counted and recounted them a hundred times, and there really were fifty, and it seemed, under the big man's fingertips, they too awakened and started living again.

Nobody had seen him enter the little church, and nobody would see him go out. Outside, the fresh air of the grey March morning brought back his hunger. He'd arrived at the village by a roundabout route, and waited until the landlord of the Mill opened up. Then he had eaten and paid for his victuals with the first of his 1,000-lire notes.

*

And now, poor man?

He put the packet of banknotes into his pocket, got up off the stump and started slowly walking. He found a cart track and all the way along it, keeping his head down, he continued to think about the 590 lire at the pub and the price tags in the outfitter's window and shoemaker's shop. A pair of shoes, a suit, a hat and a few clothes. And then, if he was lucky, ten, or fifteen, or twenty meagre meals at the most, and that would be the end of his treasure. And what about sleeping? And smoking? And the rest?

Suddenly it was as if he had been dealt a great hammer blow on the head: he stood there trembling in shock. But it was the sound of the church bell, for the church stood but twenty metres away. Subsequent chimes served to calm him, and he stopped thinking about the 590 lire and the rest. He thought instead about the church and the bell, and wandered back and forth for quite a while along the cart track, which came to an end behind the church, in front of the orchard hedge.

'Who knows if he'll still be here?' the man asked himself. And then he saw him, bigger and broader than ever, still with his cassock unbuttoned over his belly, still with his outrageous, shapeless old hat, still with a Tuscan medium held between his lips.

Don Camillo came slowly along the hedge until he was face to face with the big man. He didn't have to spend long scanning the gallery of mugshots held in his brain.

'Done your time?' he asked after a few moments.

'Yes,' replied the man.

'Well, we really missed you in this land of the damned . . . Come, around through the gate.'

Don Camillo headed for the presbytery and went in, followed by the big man.

'When did you get here?'

'Last night. They took me to the city, then at four in the afternoon they let me go, and I came on foot. I have the paper.'

He handed the well-stamped sheet to Don Camillo.

'I have no interest in that. I'm not the *carabinieri*.'

He indicated a large chair, and motioned the man to sit down.

'Did you do the whole twenty-five?' he enquired.

'Twenty only: they took off five for good behaviour.'

'And now . . . how are you now?'

'I am good for nothing,' answered the big man.

His was a story so absurdly simple as to beat everything: in 1930 there'd been a nasty bust-up between twenty-five-year-old Gianni Stombarri and a certain Antonio Moletti, aged thirty – over a woman. Gianni Stombarri didn't have a lira to his name, but he did have a beautiful girlfriend. Moletti, a livestock dealer, was well-to-do but, not satisfied with that, he wanted Gianni's girlfriend too. Fists flew and one thing led to another until one morning, Moletti was found stone dead in a ditch with his head bashed in. It didn't take long for them to pick up Gianni, and in due course Gianni had to come clean: they had met by chance, and yes they'd been arguing again over the girl, then came the moment that Moletti had shoved a revolver in Gianni's face in a fury, and Gianni, to defend himself, had split Moletti's head open with the spade he was carrying over his shoulder. The facts were clear as clear could be, and they had given Gianni Stombarri twenty-five years in prison. And the big broken man in front of Don Camillo now was this Gianni Stombarri.

The big man raised his head. 'I'm the unluckiest man in the universe!' he said. 'A suit, a pair of shoes, a hat, a handful of clothes, twenty meals if I'm lucky, and that's it. This stuff cost me twenty years in jail!'

Don Camillo looked at him puzzled, and the big man took out the packet of banknotes.

'I hid these before they nabbed me, and this morning I went to get them. They were all there. Fifty 1,000-lire notes were a big deal twenty years ago . . .'

'So it *wasn't* about the girl,' said Don Camillo.

'Do I look the type to make a fool of myself over a girl? Fifty thousand lire was a big deal in 1930!' exclaimed the man.

'And now . . . I did not know anything when I was locked up. I was not thinking about anything. I was thinking only of my fifty 1,000-lire notes. I was sure I would find them when I got out. Me, I planned to buy a truck and get work . . . And now! Twenty years in jail for a suit, a pair of shoes, a hat and a handful of laundry. Nice job!'

The big man flung the packet of money onto Don Camillo's table.

'It's no use to me any more,' he said. 'Do what you want with it.'

'Take it away,' said Don Camillo, 'I don't want your filthy money!'

The man took the money and threw it in the fire. Then he stood up and left without saying a word.

And Don Camillo let him go and watched him being swallowed up by the fields.

Flesh and the Devil

IN 1950 DON Camillo's dog was called Bill, and he was a tough old beast, but in character and temperament he was the opposite of his master because he'd not be stirred to take offence even if you whacked him on the head with a hammer. He accepted the facts of life with such resignation that you'd think he had straw under his skin instead of flesh and blood. He ate if you gave him something, but you still had to say 'Eat' before he'd touch it, even when the food was right in front of him. He hated strife and had a horror of violence, and no-account little mutts could make him turn tail just by barking under his nose.

He was more like the ghost of a dog than a dog, and sometimes just to stir his self-respect and make him react to something, Don Camillo would give him a boot up the backside that would have got a man on his feet; but Bill remained unperturbed. He'd slowly turn his great head to see where this gift of God was coming from, and when he saw it was something to do with his master, he'd doze off once more. If it happened again, he might look around again; but if a third time, he just twitched his tail a bit to acknowledge receipt, since by then he'd worked out what he was dealing with.

One morning, after a night of heavy snow, Don Camillo came out of the presbytery to clear a way from the door, and found Bill sleeping peacefully beneath a deep polar blanket of the white stuff.

To all appearances he was an idiot of a dog: and so, when Morini the butcher turned up at the presbytery in a great state to say that Bill had stolen a piece of meat weighing at least five kilos, Don Camillo burst out laughing.

'Either you've been drinking, or you dreamed it,' said Don Camillo.

But Morini hadn't been drinking or dreaming.

'I chased him all the way here,' he insisted. 'And this is where he'll be.'

They went around the house looking for Bill, and it didn't take long to find him: there he was at the end of the passage, tearing at an enormous piece of veal.

To tell the truth, Don Camillo couldn't bring himself to be outraged by this crime.

'So he's not a complete idiot after all!' he observed almost cheerfully.

'The sad part is that I'm the one who ends up looking the idiot,' responded the butcher, who had lost three or four kilos of meat.

This had to have happened on a Saturday morning, because in these parts good meat is a once-a-week luxury, and only for the very few. Indeed, for most people, beef or veal is for high days and holidays only: Christmas, Easter, the summer and autumn festivals. On those occasions the table groans with it, along with pies you need to lift with a shovel. People do eat meat at other times, but it's plainer fare: rabbits, frogs, snails, and sometimes a hen when there's a death in the henhouse, or a young cockerel when someone important comes to visit. To compensate, there is salami, boiled shoulder and cured ham, which are so amazing that if I have to be reborn as a pig, I'd pray to God to let me be born in La Bassa. (Because of the pasture, the air, the water.)

The following Saturday, Morini the butcher turned up again, puffing like the bellows of an organ: Bill had pulled the same trick, and they found him in the same place as before, but were in time to whip away the enormous piece of meat he'd stolen. Then Don Camillo, to teach him some manners, waxed lyrical with enough boots up Bill's backside to put curls on a porcupine.

And Bill took it all without a murmur; he didn't even wag his tail in acknowledgement because, with the best will in the world he couldn't have managed to count the blows.

And so along came another Saturday, and as soon as Morini had opened his shop and set out his wares, up jumped Bill from who knows where, grabbed a huge piece of meat, and fled. Morini was right behind him, but this time Bill, who remembered the storm of the previous Saturday, worked out that it was not a good idea to hide in the presbytery, and so he slipped into the passage of Barchini's house.

You have to consider that Bill was a great big dog who took a very simple view of things. Instead of snatching meat of a manageable size, he always chose the biggest piece. So, partly because he was slow by nature, and partly because it took a lot of strength just to keep the meat between his teeth, it was not out of the question, even for a man of forty-five like Morini, to run him to ground.

He caught up with Bill at the bottom of the alley by Barchini's (the stationer and printer), whipped the meat out of his mouth, and settled his account personally with a stick.

Bill came home towards evening, where the rest of his debt was paid because sin cannot be tolerated, even in a dog.

The next Saturday at five in the morning, Bill was already lying in wait, hidden behind the fountain in the piazza. As soon as Morini opened his shop and laid out the display, Bill set off at top speed and sank his teeth into the biggest piece of meat.

He fled, pursued by the butcher, who was swearing like an army of the damned: but seeing that he was about to be caught, and not wanting to lose the meat even if they killed him, Bill didn't take refuge either in the presbytery or at Barchini's. He knew now that he'd end up being chastised if he went there, so he slipped across the threshold of the local men's outfitter.

He barely had time to go in when they were onto him, taking away the meat and making him dizzy with their fury.

Leaving the shop, Bill set off towards the presbytery, but an elementary bit of reasoning stopped him half way there: in the presbytery he would be in trouble whether he turned up with or without meat. It wasn't worth his while going home, so he abandoned the piazza and opted for a life on the run.

He wandered around all day and only headed back towards the presbytery after nightfall. This is how he spent the next few days, and it was only on Thursday night, when he happened to look out of his bedroom window, that Don Camillo realised Bill was sleeping in the garden. And the priest was moved by the fact that the poor beast stayed away by day to avoid being reprimanded, while at night he felt it was his duty to come back and guard the house.

But the next Saturday came around and Bill repeated his meat-theft, this time rejecting the men's outfitters as a hiding place in favour of the chemist's shop. But even here Morini found him, took away the meat and left him very much worse for wear.

And yes, Bill did it again the following Saturday, and again for five or six Saturdays, and Don Camillo made it known publicly that he would have nothing more to do with the dog, and so people shouldn't come bothering him if Bill got up to more mischief.

Naturally Morini was determined that the dog should be stopped, and on the following Saturday, as soon as his shop was open and his meat out on display, he lay in wait armed with an iron bar: 'This time,' he thought, 'I'll break his bones and be rid of him *per omnia saecula saeculorum amen.*'[4]

And there suddenly was that damned Bill, leaping out and managing to grab a big piece of meat and make away with it before Morini could bring his iron bar to bear.

After Bill he dashed, determined to settle the matter once and for all, but the dog chose a new escape route: and this time Morini did not follow.

For here, unfortunately, politics come into play, because in that damn country by the banks of the great river, eventually *everything* turns into politics, even the mischievous doings of a dog.

Morini was one of those whom the 'Reds' call 'Blacks', and to Peppone's men he was as unwelcome as smoke in the eyes. Blows had been exchanged before between the Reds and the Blackshirts, although for now there was an uneasy truce.

Bill had found a way into the People's Palace, and Morini didn't follow him because, although he wanted to retrieve his meat, he wanted his health even more. So, he confined himself to swearing all the way back to his shop.

*

---

[4] 'Forever and ever, Amen.'

Don Camillo saw no more of Bill, and five or six weeks passed pleasantly enough before Morini once again turned up at the presbytery. He was in one of those white rages that are hot on the inside and icy on the outside: he was pale, in a cold sweat, with a tremor in his voice.

As soon as he was capable of speech, he explained himself.

'Father, this is a dirty business. I'm telling only you about it, because if I tell everyone I'll be the laughing stock of the village. This craven villainy knows no end, and I'm on the verge of doing something stupid.'

'What craven villainy?' asked Don Camillo.

'Bill!' wheezed the butcher. 'That low-life beast of yours has got me where he wants me: every Saturday he grabs the biggest piece of meat and runs to the People's Palace, and how can I get him there? You know how things are. He eats in peace, and then sits there looking out at me. He's making a fool of me. And I can't do anything about it. Those scoundrels must have worked out what's going on because I see them laughing, waiting for me to lose patience one day and come in for a shave and haircut. I'm going to end up getting a gun and shooting the dog, and that lot in the People's Palace . . . and everybody!'

Don Camillo tried to calm him down. 'There's no need to make a song and dance out of it. Just give a tip to the dog-catcher.'

'You know as well as I do that of all Peppone's Reds, the dog-catcher is the reddest.'

'The dog-catcher performs an essential public service,' exclaimed Don Camillo. 'You go to the Mayor and give him a formal petition with all the official stamps.'

'You're forgetting that the Mayor is Peppone. And there's nothing I can do because that wretched hound is never on his own; he just stays on the doorstep of the

People's Palace. The only time he goes out is when the Reds hold one of their rallies. He's always in the thick of those. At the *Festa de L'Unità* last Sunday he was marching alongside them. He's become as fat as a pig. And at my expense! And it's never going to stop!'

Morini had started to turn green and Don Camillo told him to go home and try to calm himself.

'Leave it to me,' he exclaimed firmly.

*

When Don Camillo appeared at the People's Palace, all the top brass were there: Peppone, Brusco, Bigio, Lungo, Smilzo and the rest of the gang. And so was Bill, and as soon as the dog saw Don Camillo, he lifted his nose and then crouched in a corner behind Peppone.

'They told me that dog was here,' said Don Camillo. 'I've come to take him back. He's mine.'

Peppone looked at him.

'*Your* dog? Haven't you been telling everybody that you were no longer answering for your dog?'

'That may be so,' retorted Don Camillo, 'but don't you sometimes retract things you say? . . . The fact is, the dog is mine.'

Peppone held out his arms. 'If he's yours, how come he's been living here for ages?'

'For the simple reason that he follows the golden rule for fugitives. Whoever's up to no good knows a good hiding place.'

Peppone turned red: he clearly knew the whole Morini story and would like nothing better than to play it to advantage.

'I warn you, we don't tolerate provocation,' he cried banging his fist against the table. 'If you try throwing your weight around here, you'll get the worst of it. This can be a very rough place, Father.'

Don Camillo was unperturbed. 'I don't think you're well, comrade Peppone,' he said. 'Go and see the doctor. You must have a bit of liver trouble. Or maybe a touch of Korea...'[5]

Peppone wanted to say a lot of things in response to this, but he became so highly agitated that the veins of his neck swelled to look like sausages and he was unable to utter a word.

Finally he yelled, 'Take your dog, and clear off out of here!'

Don Camillo turned to the dog. 'Come on, Bill!' he said.

But the dog did not move.

'Come on!' repeated Don Camillo. And since the dog still did not move, the priest advanced towards him. And then, like Peppone, Bill tensed and stretched ready to snap, and started growling threateningly, baring his teeth.

'Stop, or he'll tear you to pieces!' cried Smilzo.

Bill did look truly frightening, and Don Camillo pressed him no further.

'I hadn't realised,' said Don Camillo to Peppone. 'I didn't know he'd become one of yours, and taken the party card. You can see he's in his element.'

Peppone came round from behind the table and planted himself in front of Don Camillo.

'What do you mean by "element"?' he asked through clenched teeth.

'I simply meant that a dog, finding himself amongst dogs like himself, feels happier than in the house of a priest.'

---

[5] As Guareschi was writing the Korean War (1950–1953) had become the violent focus of the Cold War between the West and Soviet Russia. Don Camillo's pun on Korea/chorea (a debilitating neurological disease) was always bound to get Peppone's goat.

Peppone couldn't restrain himself and raised his fist threateningly at Don Camillo. And then something scary happened – howling like an enraged wolf, Bill snapped and lunged at Peppone, and no one could pull the dog off, so Peppone would have been torn to pieces if Lungo hadn't pulled a pistol out of his pocket and fired.

After the shot, a long, heavy silence.

Everyone stood looking at Bill, who was sprawled on the floor twitching. Even Peppone stood looking at him, stunned, the blood flowing from the wounds that Bill's teeth had inflicted on him quite unnoticed.

When Bill stopped moving, Don Camillo looked up.

'One day the people you are deceiving will understand your real intentions and will turn against you, like Bill. But the people are not Bill are they? And Lungo's pistol will not save you.'

Don Camillo left, but didn't go straight back to the presbytery. Instead he took to the fields. Evening fell and he continued to wander alone amidst the deserted flat-lands, all the time feeling the shadow of Bill tracking him, faithful into eternity.

Pio and the Cow

THE BARGHINI FAMILY all came into the world with a few marbles missing, and Pio della Pioppetta was, *inter alia*, a Barghini.

Pio Barghini had five or six good beasts in the barn, and the best of them was the Rossa, a world-beating cow, remarkable both for her milk and her work. Again, she was such a beautiful beast that it was a pity to keep her shut up in the barn for any length of time, so one day Pio put her, instead of the mare, between the shafts of his cart and drove her around the village: a sight that had people bust a gut laughing.

When the First War broke out, Pio wasn't worried: people in the village were losing sleep for fear of the call to arms, but Pio went on as calmly as ever because all that mattered to him was that they didn't call up cows, and that they'd leave him his Rossa.

However, one day a hellish and misbegotten machine that had either got lost or wanted a bit of fun, flew over the village and dropped a bomb. And the bomb landed right on the Rossa who was grazing. It didn't explode, but it hit her full on the head.

Everyone was tightening their belts and meat was as precious as gold, but Pio buried the cow and stood guard over her tomb for a fortnight because he understood that a cow as exceptional as the Rossa had the right to be treated not as an animal but as a Christian. No one could drag him away from his vigil.

Having got over his grief, Pio's thoughts turned once more to business. Beside himself with rage, he went straight to the local podestà.[6]

'You are in charge,' said Pio. 'You people wanted this war, so you pay for my cow.'

The Podestà replied that he should make a proper list of damages, according to the rules. And Pio made a list and waited, but he never saw a tin cent.

He went to complain to the Podestà five or six times, and five or six times the Podestà shrugged and flung out his arms. So, Pio took a big sheet of foolscap paper and wrote to the King: 'I beseech you to reimburse me for the loss of my cow which was bombed to death because of the war.'

After a month they sent for him at the Town Hall and told him to make a new copy of the document, because there were people interested in his cow in Rome. And Pio repeated his request.

Weeks and months went by, and nothing happened at all.

'All that bloke cares about is the war, and he doesn't give a dried fig for my cow!' said Pio one day, looking at the portrait of the King hanging in the kitchen. And from that moment his rage grew until, a few months later, he kicked the portrait of the King into the cesspit.

His hatred grew and he started publicly yelling 'Down with the King! Death to the King!' and worse stuff, though always against the King. For a while they

---

[6] Podestà was a non-elected local office, similar to Mayor and appointed by royal decree after Mussolini abolished mayoral elections in 1926. But the first documented usage of 'podestà' was in Bologna in 1151.

pretended not to hear him because Pio was a Barghini, and even the cats knew that the Barghinis came into the world with a few marbles missing.

But one thing led to another, and one fine day the *carabinieri* came and took him, but he wasn't charged with anything because it was instantly clear that his brain had turned and that Pio was stark raving mad.

In the asylum, Pio della Pioppetta behaved like a perfect gentleman: because Pio *was* a gentleman, and if he hadn't had this obsession with the King, there would have been no reason to keep him shut up with the mad men.

But the obsession was there, and every now and then he'd start shouting 'Down with the King! Death to the King!' and so on, and nobody could shut him up. He went on shouting 'Down with the King!' all through the Second War, and even after it was over. And so time passed, until one fine morning the director of the asylum said Pio should be sent home.

'Now that we're a Republic, shouting "Down with the King!" doesn't make you a madman, but a patriot,' the director explained.

And so Pio was sent home. Back in the village, his life resumed its tranquil path, and every so often people would hear him shout against the King. And so the wheel of time turned for a couple of years until one day Peppone, hearing Pio shouting, 'Death to the King!' outside his workshop, pulled him in and tried to reason with him.

'Pio, why do you keep shouting "Down with the King!"?'

Pio gave him a dirty look. 'You know perfectly well why. The King is a scoundrel who makes wars and doesn't pay me for my cow!'

Peppone spread his arms. 'It's a waste of breath, Pio, shouting "Down with the King!" when there isn't any king . . . No More King.'

Pio was astonished. 'So where's he gone?'

'He's dead.'

'When one king dies they make another one,' said Pio. 'Makes no difference whether it's the old one or a new one, it's still the same damned filthy gang who make wars and don't pay for cows.'

'There aren't any more kings,' explained Peppone. 'The monarchy ended quite a while ago. It's a Republic now.'

'Balle!' cried Pio.

So Peppone went to find some papers with the emblem of the Republic stamped on them, and Pio, who was only mad when talking about his cow and the king, was convinced.

'So, how does this Republic work then?' he asked.

'Instead of a king, there's a citizen elected by the people. One like you and me, in fact.'

Pio looked at him in amazement.

'If it's someone like you and me, what's the point of him?'

'He does what a king does. He signs sealed papers, opens monuments, welcomes dignitaries from abroad, sends telegrams when someone important dies, and so on.'

'If he just does what a king does, where's the advantage over a king?'

'The advantage is that the President isn't hereditary. After seven years we vote again, and if he isn't any good, we change him.'

'Seven years is a long time!'

'And if a damned king hangs around for ninety years and then hands over to a son even worse than he is, wouldn't that be worse?'

Pio pondered this.

'I don't know,' he answered. 'I'd have to try it out.'

But Peppone continued to pursue his point in the most beautiful personable manner, along the lines: given this is how things were, why go on being angry with someone who's not there any more?

His reasoning seemed to make a deep impression on Pio, who headed to the exit with his head bowed. When he was at the door, he turned: 'And this president you're talking about,' he asked, 'does he pay for cows?'

'Of course,' replied Peppone. 'You make your request for compensation, specify the damages, and then the Republic pays the money.'

'Do I still have to go to the Podestà?'

'No, there's no Podestà either. Now it's the Mayor.'

Pio came back. 'And what's a Mayor?'

'He's a kind of Governor but democratic, put there by regular elections. A kind of President of the district.'

'And who is the damned good-for-nothing of a Mayor who's in charge here?'

'You're right in front of him. *I'm* the Mayor.'

Pio gave him a dirty look, but Peppone showed him some documents and convinced Pio that it wasn't a joke. Pio stared at Peppone for some time and then said: 'And who are the lowlifes who made you Mayor? Didn't they have anyone better to choose from? Aren't you Peppone the blacksmith?'[7]

'Yes, still the same.'

---

[7] Peppone is described variously as a *meccanico* (specifically a motor mechanic) and also, as here, a *fabbro* (a blacksmith).

Pio shook his head. 'This is a dodgy business,' he exclaimed. 'So, are the papers for cows now kept here in the blacksmith's workshop?'

'No, they're still in the Town Hall. The Mayor sees people there. Here, I'm Peppone the blacksmith.'

'And the Mayor who sees people there, in the Town Hall, is he the same one who works as a blacksmith here?'

'He has to be.'

Pio shook his head and sighed: 'A dodgy business.'

Then he went away, bought some official paper, wrote his request about the cow and took it to Peppone. Then, his mind at rest, he stayed at home and was no longer seen in the village. Almost a year passed before he reappeared.

One day, Peppone was working at his anvil when Pio della Pioppetta turned up at his door. Peppone stopped hammering and looked up.

'Down with the Republic!' yelled old Pio. 'Death to the Republic!'

He still hadn't been paid for his cow. And so the second wave began[8], and on every public holiday you'd hear Pio on the street or in the piazza shouting, 'Down with the Republic! Death to the Republic!' and other stuff that would bring tears to your eyes. So the *carabinieri* took him and sent him back to the asylum.

'Down with the Republic!' yelled Pio as soon as he was in front of the Director.

---

[8] Many of Guareschi's stories speak of the 'seconda ondata'. Generally this term refers to the second wave of communist purges after the first bloody 'wave' following the liberation of Italy by the Anglo-American alliance on April 25, 1945 – purges which, especially in Emilia, consumed fascists, landowners, industrialists and many priests. Fortunately, this 'second wave' never materialised.

'I understand,' replied the Director with a sigh. 'The trouble is that you're old, poor Pio, and if the monarch doesn't come back soon, you'll end your days in here.'

'Long live the King!' yelled Pio fiercely.

The Director thought hard and was about to say something to the nurse . . . Then he shook himself, 'No, no,' he exclaimed, 'let's not be silly! Take him inside and sort him out.'

The Secret Weapon

'So, WHEN ARE you going to make up your mind to come?' asked Don Camillo, taking Pinacci by the arm.

'Too late, Father,' replied Pinacci. 'At the age of fifty a man with hands that look like shovels can't start copying the alphabet like a child. And then, I have to think about my . . . troubles.'

Don Camillo wouldn't leave it there: 'And in the midst of all your troubles, there's the fact that you can neither read nor write,' he exclaimed. 'Maybe they are the worst of your troubles.'

Pinacci stated laughing.

'You're in fantasy-land, Father: you can pick up all the nonsense printed in newspapers and on posters without being able to read and write. And now, with radio, you don't even need to read either newspapers or posters.'

Pinacci was obstinate, but Don Camillo could outdo him in that.

'What do you do when you have to write a letter?'

'I *don't* write it, Father. There is enough nonsense in the world already. Why should I have to add to it? The troubles of mankind started when they invented headed notepaper.'

'But what if somebody *sends* you a letter?'

'I get someone to read it to me.'

'And what if this letter has things in it that you don't want other people to know about?'

Pinacci spread his arms. 'I don't have any dirty business to worry about. I am clean, my affairs are clean: anyone can know about them.'

'You've got a head like cast iron!' cried Don Camillo. 'One day your obstinacy will get you into trouble, and then I'll be the one laughing at you!'

Pinacci shook his head. 'You won't laugh, Father, because I know you, and I know you've never laughed at a poor wretch in trouble. Leave me in my ignorance. We unfortunates are like a person with a stomach as small as a nut: as long as he only has a little to eat, he's hungry but he stays well and keeps going. The day someone gives him a pot of ravioli and a turkey, at last he's not hungry any more . . . but it kills him.

'Father, I know what can fit into my head. If I learn to read I'll learn a load of other stuff, and in two months my brain will be swamped and it'll turn me stupid. There is no Commandment saying you have to learn the alphabet.'

But fate had it that Don Camillo should see Pinacci again very soon. Less than a week later he appeared at the presbytery.

'Have you made a momentous decision?' asked Don Camillo.

But Pinacci had not. He pulled a letter from his pocket and handed it to Don Camillo.

'It came this morning, Father. I need you to read it to me.'

'And why should I be the one to read it? Is this the first time you've received a letter?'

'It's the first time I've received a letter like this one. I've always had open letters: postcards, tax forms, letters with the stamp of the Town Hall or the Government. This one is sealed, and that means only I need to know what it says. And since priests hear everything and say nothing, I've come to you.'

Don Camillo took the letter, opened the envelope and took out the paper. And as soon as he'd unfolded it he banged his fist on the table.

Pinacci looked at him in astonishment.

'What is it?' he stammered.

'Nothing,' answered Don Camillo.

Pinacci was bewildered. Don Camillo, meanwhile, pored over the letter some more:

'It would have been better if you had burned it,' he explained finally. 'This is an imbecile amusing himself by insulting people. He says you're a thief, a swindler, and so on.'

In fact, the letter was not about Pinacci: it was about his daughter. And it was slandering her so as to deal a nasty blow to her sensitive father as well. All lies, of course, but calumny is a breeze that likes to build into a hurricane and turn the heads of even the most imperturbable people.

Pinacci was thoroughly perplexed even by what Don Camillo had told him. 'Why's he saying I'm a thief and a swindler?'

'Because he's a wretch who enjoys offending people by insulting them. I'll read it to you word for word: "Dear Signor Francesco Pinacci, since no one has had the courage to tell you that you are a thief, I will . . ."' Don Camillo went on, pretending to read, and trying to come up with insults of a more general kind.

'And the signature?' asked Pinacci. 'Tell me who it is and I'll go round to his house and smash his head in.'

Don Camillo slapped his hand against the letter. 'Haven't I made it clear to you that this was written by a dirty coward?' he yelled. 'What kind of signature do you expect? It's an anonymous letter and just signed "Someone who knows everything". If we knew who the swine was, I'd soon cure him of his interest in writing anonymous letters. I dare say there are quite a few people who'd like to give him a smack on the head!'

Pinacci was upset and Don Camillo tried to cheer him up by saying, 'Don't think any more about it, he's just a trouble-maker. You have a clear conscience and if someone insults you anonymously, it cannot touch you. Just leave the letter here so that I can study the handwriting.'

*

When Pinacci had gone, Don Camillo opened a drawer and took out another eleven letters. He was not mistaken: the writing was the same. Eleven other people had received a letter from the damned wretch "who knows everything" and all of them, after reading the anonymous slanders, had secretly come to consult the priest. And Don Camillo had worked feverishly to try and calm them down and convince them not to take seriously the filth contained in the letters. They were all charges against wives, fiancées or daughters. Detailed accusations, put together with extraordinary skill, by someone with a deep knowledge of his victims. It had to be someone from the neighbourhood.

This dirty business of the anonymous letters had been gnawing at Don Camillo's vitals for quite a while now, but what could he do? The letters had been entrusted to him on condition of the utmost secrecy, so there was no question of informing the Marshal of the *Carabinieri*.

'I just wish this wretch would write one to me,' thought Don Camillo. 'Then I could really give him what's coming to him!'

But no letter came. A fortnight after Pinacci's letter, Peppone turned up. He appeared in front of the presbytery, where Don Camillo was sitting on the bench by his door smoking a half cigar.

'May one respectfully ask,' said Peppone with great solemnity, 'if the parish priest is at leisure to receive the Mayor on business of great public importance?'

Don Camillo looked at him in astonishment, stood up, went into the presbytery and then appeared at the window. 'The parish priest says that the Mayor may come in.'

Once inside, Peppone insisted Don Camillo close the door and all the windows before getting down to the matter in hand.

'There's a scoundrel in this village having fun writing anonymous letters,' said Peppone. 'I've received one, and so have fifteen other people whose names don't concern you. Anyway, here they all are.'

Peppone pulled a bundle out of his pocket and presented the letters to Don Camillo.

Then Don Camillo fetched his own clump of letters from a drawer, took one out of its envelope, and folded it so that only four or five lines were visible.

'Let's see,' he muttered.

Peppone did the same with one of his letters and the two were placed side by side on the table.

'It is the same wretch,' concluded Don Camillo after a brief examination. 'So, you just need to take the letters to the Marshal . . .'

'Why do *you* not do it?'

'Because a priest may hear everything, but cannot divulge any of it. It's different for the Mayor.'

Peppone rubbed his chin.

'The trouble is that these letters weren't entrusted to me as Mayor, but as let's say. . .'

'Don't tell me: they've been entrusted to you in your capacity as head of the fifth column, or some such. But you can still do what you want with the letter sent to you. It's yours, *you* were sent it, and you have only yourself to answer to.'

Peppone shook his head, 'You're mistaken, Father. I have to answer to the Party. I have been slandered privately, and if I make it public I'll do harm to myself and therefore to the Party.'

'And how are you going to make it public? The Marshal isn't going to print your letter on his posters! He'll keep it to himself!'

'Where power over another is put in the hands of a public official it is never going to remain a private matter; it is always eventually made public. And see here, Father, there are things in this letter, so many things concerning my family's most private affairs, that I'd rather eat it than have it read by another!'

'Well, all right then,' replied Don Camillo. 'Let's agree, if I learn anything about this business I'll pass it on to you. And if you hear something, you tell me.'

Don Camillo already had an idea:

'The Strada Quarta dyke is something that's troubling everyone – on both sides of the political divide. People are scared that it'll break at the first high water. Send some of your hooligans to get your people to organise a petition to send to the Government – all males over fifteen must write, "I agree with the above," and add their signature. Meanwhile, I'll draw up the same kind of petition and go around collecting the signatures of everyone else. Then we'll have samples of everyone's handwriting. We can get down to studying it, and something will surely be revealed.'

*

Don Camillo started his campaign two days later, and it was a hard job because, first of all, he had to explain what was needed, and then explain it again, and if the men weren't at home he had to come back, or hunt for them in the fields. On the third day, completely worn out, he found himself out in the countryside with a puncture. He flung himself disconsolately down onto the grass, but – thank the Lord! – an ox cart soon came into view. It was full of sugar beet and heading for the little town, where trucks were waiting to load up with beets for processing into sugar in the city.

And at the front of the wagon . . . was Pinacci.

'I've been reduced to walking,' Don Camillo said to him. 'Let me load my bike on your cart and come up beside you because I'm tired to death.'

A few moments later Don Camillo was sitting beside Pinacci. 'I'm collecting signatures about the Strada Quarta dyke,' he explained. 'That means I'm getting a sample of everyone's handwriting. I'll catch the rascal who wrote you that letter, you'll see!'

Pinacci clenched his fists. 'If you tell me who he is just before you tell the rest, you'll be doing me a favour. I'll teach them what's what.'

The cart went slowly along the road and arrived at the bend and the wooden bridge over the big canal. At the opening onto the bridge a large notice had been nailed to a post: 'Warning! Danger of Death! Weak Bridge. No Access for Vehicles over 500 Kilos.'

'What's that writing?' asked Pinacci. 'It wasn't there yesterday.'

'Nothing to worry about,' replied Don Camillo after reading the notice. 'One of those advertisements for shaving soap. They're even going up in the countryside now.'

Pinacci nodded and touched the oxen with a whip, and they continued on their way.

The cart ventured onto the bridge – one metre, two metres, three metres, five metres – and its boards started to creak under the heavy cart's wheels.

'Now,' considered Don Camillo, 'I could tell him the truth and make him die of fright. That would teach him the dangers of not knowing how to read!'

. . . Six metres, seven metres, fifteen metres . . .

Another five metres and the wheels would be making planks groan that certainly wouldn't withstand the weight of the cart. And it really was time to stop because, to tell the truth, Don Camillo's legs were already beginning to anticipate the cold . . .

At that very moment, Pinacci yelled 'Who-o-o-o-oa!' and the oxen stopped.

Don Camillo looked at him. 'Well? Why do you not go on?'

'Because I can read,' said Pinacci, scowling.

It was no easy matter getting the cart to shift into reverse gear and go fifteen metres backwards, but they managed it in the end. They took a different route, by the Molinetto bridge. At the acacia thicket Don Camillo made Pinacci stop the cart, dragged him off it, grabbed him by the neck and started to squeeze.

'I learned to read when I was in the army. I never told anyone because it was handy for me to make people think I was an idiot,' stammered Pinacci.

'And you learned to write too. So why did you write a letter to yourself as well?'

'I was afraid someone from the village might have seen me posting some of the letters . . . But you can't say anything because what I'm telling you is under the seal of the confessional.'

'Of course,' said Don Camillo calmly. 'It is just between you and me.'

The first kick that visited Pinacci weighed three tons, then it was balanced by a slap of equal weight, followed by a hurricane of slaps and kicks.

Pinacci began to moan.

'Now,' explained Don Camillo, 'I have to give you the ones you owe the Mayor.'

So Pinacci ended up taking all the blows due to the entire town council, and they came with the force of such a cyclone that the good Lord Jesus put his hands in front of his eyes so as not to see.

The Bribe

NEVER TAKE A peasant's money. When you do something for him and he anxiously asks how much he owes you, do not say, 'A thousand lire.' Instead, tell him you don't want money but a token of some sort by way of payment. Ask him if he could sort that out for you and he'll give you all kinds of stuff to the value of 5,000 lire and will thank you with tears in his eyes.

Never touch a peasant's money: let him bury it in some vessel that'll preserve it. Let him complain endlessly about his poverty. Ultimately, it's as if his buried money doesn't exist. It is as if the State had not printed those notes.

*

On the altar steps, Don Camillo found a package tied up with string and on it an address written in indelible pencil, which read: 'To Jesus Christ'. Inside the package there were one hundred 1,000-lire banknotes and a letter: 'Jesus, my father is in a fury as if possessed by devils. I am sending you this money so that you will make him better.'

A week went by and one morning Don Camillo found another package, like the first containing one hundred 1,000-lire notes, and a similar letter asking grace for the 'possessed father'.

The extraordinary request was repeated the following week, and on two further occasions, seven days apart, Don Camillo found the package addressed to Jesus, with the letter and the notes, each worth 1,000 lire, once again on the altar steps.

'Jesus,' said Don Camillo finally, 'this is beginning to disturb me. We have now reached 500,000 lire and I have not slept for a long time. I don't know how my poor head will cope if I find another package in a week's time with the letter and more money.'

*

It was starting to get dark when the little boy set off on the road through the fields. After walking for a while beside a hedge, he jumped over a ditch and came upon a large elm. The fields were deserted and the January mist made the scene yet more bleak and silent.

The boy of ten or eleven, bundled up in a man's jacket and with a woollen cap on his head, sat down at the foot of the great elm. He cleared aside some stones and started to dig away at the earth with a stick. After a while he felt something hard, so he chucked the stick aside, began digging with his hands and unearthed an upside-down jar, which he carefully pulled out. The jar was acting as a kind of hood over a short green glass bottle protected with a piece of waterproof canvas like a carboy, and sealed with a stopper heavily greased so as prevent the ingress of any moisture whatever. The boy took the stopper out of the bottle, which was now out of the ground, slipped a wire hook down inside it and started to wiggle it around. When he felt it catch onto something, he pulled it out, bringing with it a little roll covered in oiled paper and secured with tape.

'Damn you, you little swine!' someone shouted at that moment. The small boy jumped up and tried to run away, but was instantly blocked by the tines of a three-pronged pitchfork. It was old Sisto, watching him with his piggy eyes. 'If you make a dumb move I'll skewer you,' he said through clenched teeth. The little boy felt the points of the fork pressing on his chest and the great trunk of the elm behind him.

'I haven't done anything,' he stammered.

'Where did you put the other five?' demanded old Sisto.

'It wasn't me,' answered the boy. 'I only took what's there on the ground . . . I found the bottle open and I looked to see what was inside.'

Old Sisto pushed the fork against the boy's chest: 'Dirty little swine,' he gasped. 'I've been watching you for three days from behind those posts. I saw you arrive and dig. And it was you who took the five missing rolls!'

'I never took nothing . . . I don't know what you're talking about,' whispered the boy.

'Yes you do!' shouted the old man. 'If it hadn't come to me three days ago that I should dig up the bottle and count the rolls, you'd have robbed me of the lot! Where've you put the other five? Tell me or I'll skewer you!'

'I don't know nothing! It wasn't me!' insisted the little boy. Old Sisto was beside himself: he ground his teeth and shoved his fork viciously against the boy's skinny chest. 'I'll skewer you!' he panted.

At that moment a gunshot from a huntsman in the vicinity made old Sisto jump and turn his head. The little boy slipped away, but a point of the fork caught his left arm and tore the flesh.

'I'll see you later!' shouted the old man after him.

*

His arm was hurting terribly, but the little boy made out that nothing was wrong when he got home. He tied it up as best he could with his handkerchief and since it was dinner time sat down at the table. His mother poured him out a ladleful of soup straight away.

'Cino, eat that up right now,' she said, taking off his cap. 'You must have got frozen. You're white as a sheet.'

The boy started eating in silence, and a little later his father arrived.

Cino Delpiò's father was little more than thirty, a huge man with arms like beams of oak, yet he had an old man's face – weary, with deep wrinkles. He threw his hat into a corner and sat at the table.

'I've told you before, we begin to eat *only* when I come home!' said the man. 'I'm sick to death of saying the same thing over and over!'

'The boy was chilled to the bone, and really not well,' his wife explained deferentially.

'Nobody obliges him to stay out all day long, hanging about on the street!' the man replied roughly.

He stank of wine, and tears came into the woman's eyes: the demons had him, the poor creature – this was no longer the man she'd known so well.

Just then they heard the door creaking, and old Sisto appeared. He had his shotgun under his arm and his face was grimmer than ever.

'Give me back my money!' said the old man.

The husband and wife looked at him in amazement.

'Money? What money?' stammered the boy's father.

'I caught your son stealing my money. Five rolls, one hundred 1,000-lire notes in each one. He took them. Hand them over or there'll be trouble.'

The boy's father couldn't work out what was going on.

'Sisto,' he protested, 'have you gone right off your head?'

'There's nothing wrong with my head,' shouted the old man. 'And there's not going to be. Either you give me my 500,000 lire back right now, or I go to the Marshal and have you charged. You two are responsible for that boy. And for all I know, it was you who put him up to this. I'll have you thrown in jail!'

The boy looked up: 'It wasn't them,' he said, 'I took the money.'

The woman turned pale and her husband leapt to his feet.

'You took the money?' he yelled, grabbing the boy by his hair.

'Yes,' replied the boy calmly. 'I found it in a bottle under the elm. I didn't know it was his.'

Old Sisto intervened. 'Where've you put my money?' he yelled.

'I don't remember,' said the boy. 'I didn't know it was money . . . I found it under the tree . . .'

His father, still holding him tightly by his hair, pulled him off his chair: 'Tell us, you little villain. Say where you put it, or I'll kill you! If you don't talk, you'll ruin me, understand? Where did you put that money?'

'I don't remember,' answered the boy.

Carlo Delpiò's hands were massive and heavy, and the boy was slender and fragile. The woman threw herself screaming onto the boy to protect him from the horrendous blows and, for one moment, the man's fury switched to his wife.

'Get out of the way, you!' yelled Carlo, grabbing the woman and sending her flying into a corner of the kitchen.

The little boy's face was covered in blood, and when his father's hands took hold of him again he thought he'd soon be dead, but he carried on repeating, 'I don't know . . . I don't know . . . I can't remember.'

And then the man felt as if he had nothing but a bit of rag in his hands, which frightened him, so he let the boy go. His son flopped to the floor, while he turned to old Sisto and said, 'I cannot break his neck.'

'You put on a nice show,' answered the old man coldly. 'I want my money back, and I'll have it.'

Cino was a little stick of a boy, but he had the thick skin of a Delpiò. He came to while his father was yelling at old Sisto, slipped through the door, and vanished into the night.

*

That evening Don Camillo couldn't re-read his old numbers of the *Sunday Courier* in peace, because for some reason his dog, Ful, was very agitated. He kept growling and watching the door suspiciously, so in the end Don Camillo got his shotgun and opened the door to see what on earth could be hiding behind it. The passageway was deserted, but now Ful was giving his close attention to the door that gave onto the kitchen garden. So Don Camillo opened this one too. Once in the garden, Ful headed straight for the woodshed, and Don Camillo saw something moving amongst the bundles of logs.

He lit the lamp in the porch. Ful went and stuck his nose into the logs, and once he was certain that this was nothing that could interest a hunting dog and nothing that could concern a guard dog, he calmly returned to Don Camillo's feet.

'Out you come!' thundered Don Camillo. But when he saw little Delpiò standing in front of him with his face beaten to a pulp, he regretted yelling.

At that moment, someone banged on the front door and Don Camillo went to see who it was, after saying to the boy: 'Wait here and don't move, or the dog will tear you to pieces.'

It was Barchini, his number one informant, who had come to bring him the evening's news:

'A terrible thing, Father,' said the printer, 'Old Sisto's had half a million stolen from him, and it seems it was the little Delpiò boy, together with his parents. At any rate, the *carabinieri* have already been called in.'

Once Barchini had gone, Don Camillo went to fetch the little Delpiò from the shed, and took him into his sitting room.

'Who was the brute who made such a mess of your face?' he asked as he mopped the boy's face with a wet towel.

'Nobody,' replied the boy. 'I fell over.'

Don Camillo grabbed him by the arm and the boy let out a groan. So Don Camillo took off his jacket, saw the wound made by the fork, and became even angrier.

'And who did this to you?' he asked.

'Nobody,' answered the boy. 'When I fell over. . . there was a nail in a floorboard . . .'

Don Camillo disinfected the wound and bandaged it up.

'What's this story about money stolen from old Sisto?' asked Don Camillo.

'I don't know,' replied the boy.

'So the *carabinieri* will put your father and mother in prison,' insisted Don Camillo.

'No,' said the boy, 'It's got nothing to do with them. I found the money in a bottle.'

'And where did you put it?'

'I don't know. I didn't know it was money. I thought it was just stuff to play with.'

'So you played with those pieces of paper!'

'Yes.'

'With your peashooter, maybe. You made them into pellets for your peashooter, which means you fired them who knows where.'

'Yes.'

'Maybe you fired them at a target that was in the river.'

'Yes,' agreed the boy. 'The water took them all away. I remember now.'

'Are you hungry? Are you thirsty?'

'No.'

'Sleepy?'

The boy shook his head, but his eyes were closed and he was already falling asleep on the sofa. Don Camillo covered him with his cloak, and then instructed Ful:

'Stay there and if he wakes, tell him I'm coming straight back.'

Ful gave him a look as if to say that, when you came down to it, all men are a bit soft in the head.

*

Carlo Delpiò was alone in his kitchen. Alone in the blackest of moods. His wife was sobbing in bed upstairs.

'Who beat up your boy like that?' asked Don Camillo.

'I did!' shouted the man, jumping to his feet in a rage. 'Why?'

'So,' said Don Camillo, 'a nice piece of work.'

'He ruined me!' shouted the man. 'He stole 500,000 lire from Sisto, and won't say where he put them.'

Don Camillo took some notes out of his pocket and laid them on the table in front of Carlo. 'Five packets with a hundred 1,000-lire notes in each of them arrived addressed to Jesus Christ, and with this letter inside,' he explained.

The man read the letters, open-mouthed.

'As you see, all this is really your fault.'

The man jumped up. 'But everything's all right now! All I have to do is explain . . .'

'All you have to do is keep quiet,' replied Don Camillo. 'I'll do the talking.'

The Marshal of the *Carabinieri* arrived with two of his men and old Sisto.

'The boy stole it together with them,' said old Sisto darkly. 'They must have hidden it somewhere. You have to find it!'

'Where's the boy?' asked the Marshal.

'At my house,' explained Don Camillo. 'He's still in shock. He told me how things went. He thought it was just any old paper, and used it for playing with his peashooter. His parents know nothing about it.'

'That's easy to say, but hard to prove,' responded the Marshal doubtfully.

'I don't think so,' replied Don Camillo. 'What would these people want with worthless scraps of paper?' The Marshal looked at Don Camillo dumbfounded.

'Marshal,' said Don Camillo, 'Question this old imbecile. Get him to tell you how many 1,000-lire notes there were in the bottle, for example . . .'

Old Sisto protested, 'No I don't tell anyone about my private business!'

'How much money was in the bottle?' asked the Marshal. 'I have to know.'

Old Sisto muttered, 'Twenty . . .'

'Twenty what?'

'Twenty rolls like this,' he said, pulling out of his pocket the roll which the boy had fished out of the bottle a few hours before.

The Marshal took off the waxed paper and counted the 1,000-lire notes. 'One hundred?'

'Yes, twenty rolls of a hundred.'

'Two million lire,' the Marshal went on. 'Of which you still have a million and a half!'

'Yes, but I want the rest back, it's mine!'

'True,' replied the Marshal, 'but two million or one and a half, it's all the same, because this money is only fit for turning into beer!'

'Beer?' stammered the old man. 'What do you mean, beer?'

'These are Am-Allied Military Currency – AM-lire – wartime lire,[9] and they haven't been legal tender for years. They're worthless.'

Old Sisto protested that he didn't know, nobody had ever told him, he didn't read the nonsense in the papers and kept himself to himself.

'Consider the two million that you're ahead,' Don Camillo consoled him. 'You don't need that money! Okay, if you'd earned it through hard work, it would be a sad loss, but since you got it through the black market, what does it matter?'

Old Sisto was in despair, but the Marshal found another angle to console him: 'You've done the Government an excellent service by getting rid of this paper. You're a worthy ally in the battle against inflation.'

*

Left alone with Delpiò, Don Camillo lit his cigar. 'Everyone thinks your son used those banknotes for his peashooter. Nobody needs to know what really happened.'

'Yes,' said the man. Then he re-read the letters and kept on saying, 'Why does he say I've been possessed?'

---

[9] Currency issued in Italy by the Allied Military Government for Occupied Territories following the Allied invasion of Sicily in 1943. 100 AM-lire were worth 1 US dollar.

'Don't worry about it,' Don Camillo responded reassuringly. 'Maybe Jesus will enlighten you and explain it. Jesus shares your son's opinion. He's taken his bribe. Defunct US army lire they may be, but Jesus will take them as good currency. He won't know the difference.'

Don Camillo went home and the little boy was no longer asleep on the sofa. He was in the church, kneeling before Jesus. Don Camillo stood behind a confessional box and listened to the boy saying, 'Jesus, even if he'd stuck the fork into me, I would never have told him I gave you the money to make my dad better. Don't worry, nobody in the whole world will ever know, even if they kill me.'

And then he heard Jesus answer, 'All right, Cino, I'll see what I can do to help you . . .'

And he had already helped him, as Don Camillo knew for sure.

The Agriculturalist

NOBODY COULD EVER understand how old Piletti became the owner of three *biolca* of land.

Long ago, a piece of the Carossa estate had become separated from the rest when they made the Strada Nuova. It was a slice of land measuring about ten thousand square metres which was nothing but a headache for the family at Carossa and no use to the neighbouring estate because a stream ran through the middle of it. In any case, it was a scrap of land fit for nothing, and had never had a use before; just a mine of rocks that yielded only couch grass.

So, when Piletti, who was then a 22-year-old day labourer with not a penny to his name, had told the proprietors of Carossa that he was willing to work the land in his spare time, they said, 'Take it and have fun with it.'

Piletti had a grand plan in his head, and put his shoulder to the wheel: 'All right,' he said, 'but since I've got something big in mind, I want a guarantee that the land stays in my name for twenty-five years.'

At these words, old Gradelli the owner of Carossa, became suspicious, so he called his three sons and went to make a careful inspection of the strip of land between the Strada Nuova and the stream. All four brought spades: they tested the ground in every part, and found nothing but stone. And the more they dug the more stones they found.

Finally the old man concluded, 'This bloke's crazy. But since only a mad man could get anything out of this rubbish, let's give him the twenty-five year contract.'

But Piletti wasn't crazy: rather, his brain was so structured as to be averse to forming imaginative representations of things that bore no relation to reality. He was both a realist and a hard worker. So, he got down to work before the ink was even dry on the contract. First he dug a big ditch nearly three metres across, which divided the piece of land lengthwise into two. It took months and months, and every so often the family from Carossa would come to stare in astonishment at the enormous trench, eventually two metres deep, and at the mountain of rocky spoil being heaped up on either side.

When the trench was finished, the young man nailed a piece of wire mesh onto a wooden frame, grabbed a shovel, spat on his hands, and began to sieve the soil dug from the trench. And he threw the biggest stones into the trench, and this job also took an enormous quantity of time, but the young man had a brain undistracted by fantasy and he never lost patience.

When the work was finished, Piletti started to clean the earth off other stones and, one cart-load at a time, he threw them into the trench. And when he had cleaned up a quarter of the field, he brought to it the earth dug out of the trench. In the end, the enormous trench was filled up with a dusting of the smaller stones and a bumpy track became a broad and comfortable cart track.

Piletti had to do all this work after slaving elsewhere to keep body and soul together, and so he took his time over it: but he had twenty-five years ahead of him and calmly soldiered on.

He divided the land into lots and set to work on thoroughly improving the first of them, digging out more stones and throwing them into the river. Then, when he heard that somewhere else nearby they were digging foundations for a house, he went to collect the earth from there and filled the holes left by the stones.

The Good Lord, it has to be said, helped him greatly, because the girl Piletti had married in the meantime not only brought him the assistance of two solid arms, but also a horse and cart, her entire inheritance from her recently deceased father, who had been a carter.

It was a slow and laborious achievement but, after five years, the piece of land started to yield something, and the family from Carossa, seeing that the business was not going badly, helped Piletti with some cartloads of manure and so on. They also allowed him to put up a hut of straw and mud, and Piletti and his wife came and lived in it.

When Piletti said to the old man from Carossa that he intended to put down some vines, the old man helped him again because, after all, he could see that this good-for-nothing was adding value to land which nobody had ever dreamed could live and bear fruit.

As the years passed, the hut was replaced by a house made of bricks, and Piletti had hens, ducks, and geese, and managed to rear a pig. Now he and his wife were living exclusively for this scrap of land, and the time that the woman had to give up when her son was born seemed to her to have been stolen from a mission, and she didn't think she could bear it.

When Piletti turned forty-seven, it was made clear to him that the contract had expired and that it would be a good idea if he got out from under their feet, because the little farm was to be put up for sale.

'Fine,' replied Piletti calmly. 'I'll buy it. I'll pay you in ten years.'

It was explained to him that such a deal was not on offer: the money was wanted right away. Old man Gradelli had died, and for his children a bird in the hand was worth two in the bush. The land was theirs: too bad that Piletti had done all that work and put up a house. The contract simply said that they guaranteed him the tenancy for twenty-five years. 'When the paperwork's right the countryman sleeps tight,' as the saying goes.

Piletti knew perfectly well that it was pointless arguing with people like that. He had some money put aside, so he went into town and bought himself a shotgun, and when the eldest of the three Carossa brothers came to tell him what they'd decided to do, Piletti showed him the gun and explained, 'I've sweated blood for this land and I'm going to defend it. You can't throw me off it: either renew the tenancy or sell me the land. I'll pay you in five years instead of ten.'

The principal owner of Carossa could see that Piletti wasn't joking. After consulting his brothers, he came back to say that they would after all sell him the land, but if he failed to complete the purchase in five years, he'd lose the lot and there'd be no arguing about it.

This brought things to the end of 1914, the start of the First War: Piletti was too old and his son too young to fight, so they both stayed home when war broke out. They worked like the damned and the value of the currency steadily fell, while the figure in the contract remained fixed. In this way Piletti was able to afford to pay for the land, which he certainly could not have done otherwise. Even so, he had to slave so hard and tighten his belt so fiercely that he couldn't have suffered more if he'd been in the trenches.

And when the war was over, all he had gained was the right to carry on working like a dog.

He went on working and day by day the little farm improved. It was a poor scrap of land, but there is no poor land in the world that can resist the efforts of a tenacious farmer.

Piletti was nursing an ambitious dream in his now old heart: a well to irrigate his land. It was a struggle but, in the end, he was able to lay some pipes. A water diviner had come and assured him that there was water twenty metres down apparently, but even at fifty there was no sign of any. Piletti was in debt up to his eyes, but he went on laying down pipes and found water at eighty-five metres.

And when the pump was installed and the water started to flow, old Piletti doffed his cap and his old wife broke down in tears.

His son left to pursue his own career, but now that there was water for irrigation, the old man felt able to achieve impossible feats. Hard labour had bent him like a sickle, but he worked like a man of forty.

When he had time to spare, he walked around his land: he knew every tiny piece of it, and there wasn't a centimetre that hadn't been bathed in his sweat. He had been working this land for sixty years, and some of the trees he had planted along the stream had majestic trunks. Old Piletti would look up and feel proud that he had built a tower that would defy the winds and the centuries. He had now reached the age of eighty-five, and the immense love he had for his scrap of land was the only thing keeping him in this world. And the old woman hung on too because, as long as the old man had the strength to keep going on his land, she had to stay alive too. She couldn't abandon him.

But then the damned oil company turned up.

*

They had been hanging around the area for some while and had opened wells a few kilometres away: but they went on exploring for more and so, one morning, they arrived at Piletti's little house and explained that they had to do some tests on his farm.

'You can't,' answered old Piletti. 'This land is mine.'

The others just laughed: 'The land is yours, but what's underneath belongs to the State. We're looking for what's underneath.'

'The land's mine on top and underneath,' insisted the old man stubbornly.

At a sign from the leader of the gang, one of them got into the van and drove off. Shortly afterwards, he came back with the Marshal of the *Carabinieri*.

'All we want is to do some tests on his land,' said the leading oil man. 'Please explain to him.'

The Marshal explained: 'This isn't a private company. They're officials from a Department of State. They have to do their jobs. This is a matter of Public Utility.'

Old Piletti went back into his house without responding. And the gang of men started roaming around his fields to organise their mischief. This went on for quite a few days, and the old man followed them at a distance, not knowing what to think.

'Jesus,' he prayed, 'don't let them find anything!'

But they did find something. They found it right there, and someone came to tell the old man to submit his request for compensation in these two formats and to these two offices, and so on and so forth. The old man didn't understand a word of it. Every so often it occurred to him to say again that the land was his, and he'd made it into a farm, bit by bit; he saw the Marshal again and heard the same words, 'Public Utility', 'the State', 'the Government' . . .

When the bloke who'd done all the explaining went away, the full size gang turned up with trucks, tractors and cranes. The little strip of land was completely churned up, and all the smaller plants flattened. It had rained shortly before and the ground was sticky: the men set up Caterpillars with steel cables hooked onto pulleys around the trunks of the trees which were knocked down, uprooted, chopped up.

A building site was set up, and the workers constructed an iron tower to drill into the ground, while trucks and tractors went to and fro continually, wrecking everything. The old couple were stuck in their house now, holed up in the attic where they watched the ruin with dismay. After a few days, the old man came down: he had to prune the vines, but he couldn't get near the building site. They ordered him away because he was causing an obstruction. He stammered some protest and got the usual replies: formal application in writing, request for compensation . . .

Passing the irrigation well, a Caterpillar got stuck and knocked a piece off the brickwork of the pump house. The old man felt his heart miss a beat. It was as if his own skull had been cracked, but the oil men took no notice. They were cursing and yelling, trying to find something to support a pulley and hawser. They decided to use the old walnut tree standing near the house, and the Caterpillar was pulled free, but the walnut tree was half uprooted.

The old couple stopped going out of the house, but in the end they were driven out of it.

By now a long time had passed, and hundreds and hundreds of metres of pipe had been planted in the heart of the earth. But either as a short cut stratagem or out of ignorance, instead of bedding it down with the right kind of mud on top of the pipe, they threw in some sort of rubbish, or they let air bubbles in, so the point came when the gas blew off the mud cap and started to flow over the ground. The gas seemed to be the breath of the Devil himself, such was the force with which it came hissing from the earth. So forceful is this gas that it can rip out bolts as if they had the consistency of porridge, and once it blows over sand it destroys everything: pipes, flanges, the lot. And it rains sand for kilometre after kilometre.

If the gas began by hissing terrifyingly out of the ground, it then caught fire, and it really seemed as if someone had opened a door into Hell. The oil gang came into the house, loaded the old couple and their few belongings onto a truck and took them to the village.

'You'll stay in these rooms until it's over,' they explained. 'Then you'll be reimbursed for the damage . . .' And so forth.

'Will it take a long time to put out the flame?' asked the old woman.

'A fortnight, a month, two, who knows? We have to drill some holes in from the side to block the main hole and then put the fire out with dynamite.'

The old couple settled as best they could into the little rooms they'd been given, and shut themselves away there for two or three days, until the old man came to a decision, and left.

And there he was standing in front of Don Camillo, who already knew the whole story.

'I want to make a protest to the Government,' said old Piletti, 'and I need you to write it for me. The land is mine, I've worked it for sixty years and more. They don't have the right to destroy my life's work and my wife's.'

'I understand, but you don't need to worry. They'll reimburse you for all your losses.'

The old man smiled sadly. 'I know that, and so do they. They come offering 20,000 lire, and if that then goes up to twenty-two it's as if they were giving you a kingdom. But even if they pay me everything I'm owed, so what? My work of sixty years has been destroyed. I haven't worked for sixty years to build a handful of dirty paper. I've given my life to a piece of dead land. A painter makes a picture: I have made that farm. A painter doesn't make a picture for you to destroy and then pay him for it. Even if you don't pay him at all, that's not the point. The point is that the picture *is still there*.'

Don Camillo tried to reason with old Piletti. 'It's a question of public benefit. We don't only work for ourselves but for others too. Out of the ground will come riches for the whole nation . . .'

The old man shook his head. 'It won't be riches for the whole nation that come out of the ground. It will be thousands of salaries for officials who produce nothing, thousands of offices, calculating machines, secretaries, and tons of official paper. And all the gas that comes out will cost people more than coal, and even so it won't cover the costs of the officials and the offices, etcetera. And the nation will have to pay new taxes. Everything the Government does always costs more than it brings in.'

Don Camillo sighed. 'Piletti, who put all this into your head? Where've you been picking up these stories?'

'I've learned them from my eighty-five years of life, Father. And you must write down on a piece of official paper everything I've just said, and then send it by express post to that lot in the Government. The land is mine, I made a farm out of it, and they are destroying all my work.'

'Don't talk nonsense, Piletti. Yes, your work has been destroyed for the public good, and that is sad and painful.

But so many people have lost their sons for the public good, and that is much more painful and sad. You should look around you before you start shouting at people.'

Old Piletti said nothing and went back to his wife.

'Well?' she asked him.

'There's nothing to be done. He told me we should thank God that our son didn't die in the war. It would be worse if we'd lost our son. And the gas is good for everyone, so we shouldn't fret about it.'

The old woman didn't fret: but now that flames were coming out of their overturned land, now that the old plants had been uprooted, now that death had repossessed their domain and the well had been dismantled and the pump had keeled over, the old woman no longer felt any moral obligation to carry on living. And so she died peacefully in the foreign land of those rooms, surrounded by her meagre belongings that were stacked like goods in a shop window.

The old man took her to the cemetery and went back to live in the rooms that were so alien also to him. He knew he couldn't do anything for his land with his two arms, but he hung on so that he could do something else.

He waited until election day.

Then presented himself at the polling station, and took his ballot paper, marched into the booth, spat on the ballot paper, folded it, and went to drop it into the box.

And this action was his spiritual legacy, because he never made it home, but died at the side of a ditch.

As a free democratic dog.

Comunque

DON CAMILLO WAS a good-natured man, and on more than one occasion had had to swallow some highly indigestible stuff: but he never quite managed to stomach Comunque.

Of all Peppone's gang, Comunque was the only one who frightened Don Camillo, and not because he was hulking or violent, but for an entirely different reason.

As long as he'd remained plain Cesarino Delfosso, he had given Don Camillo no particular cause for concern. Then, one day, Cesarino had gone off to some unknown destination to attend the Party School. He possessed a formidable memory and, coming back to the village a few months later, he was not so much a man as a perfect jukebox furnished with a complete collection of discs.

He had exactly the right record ready for anybody's objection to whatever he was saying, and each disc was cut with such diabolical cleverness that for a track or two it faithfully followed the logical thread of the discussion, before slowly, gently, without listeners noticing the shift, abandoning the subject of the objection and slipping off along a line of his own. In this way, his opponent ended up like a boxer who mounts a close guard to parry and counter the blows of an adversary standing in front of him, and suddenly gets kicked up the backside.

Besides his collection of discs, Cesarino had brought the word 'Comunque'[10] back from the city, which he had discovered at the Party School and which he liked so much that he felt the need to insert it with incredible frequency into his speech. And so, in the village he acquired the nickname 'Comunque'.

Don Camillo had been the first to experience the sneaky effectiveness of Comunque's verbal weaponry. And this was a particularly painful encounter because it took place publicly during a rally in the main square. Comunque had been speaking for some time, when Don Camillo could no longer restrain himself and made a rebuttal of some sort or other. Comunque didn't bat an eyelid, but put his *'ad hoc'* disc on the jukebox and buried Don Camillo under an avalanche of words.

'That has nothing to do with the objection I raised!' protested Don Camillo finally in reply. 'This is another matter entirely!'

Comunque only smiled. 'Once, during the war, a general went to inspect the advance guard and came upon a soldier lying stretched out on the ground. "Why aren't you standing up and saluting me?" asked the general. "I've been on guard here for eight days and no one's brought me anything to eat or drink," replied the soldier. "My question had to do with Discipline, not with Subsistence!" yelled the general. "It's an entirely different matter!"

'However,' – [or 'Comunque,' as Cesarino of course put it] – 'it is *in fact* the same matter, Father, for the simple reason that the soldier was dying of hunger and had no strength to get up and salute the general.'

---

[10] The word means 'however' or 'anyway' or 'in any case' or 'even so', and served so well Comunque's meandering, manipulative, *ad hoc*, linguistic strategy.

Don Camillo had had to fight like a lion to get himself out of that mess, and he was in pretty bad shape when he emerged, because it really *is* impossible to argue with a jukebox.

Comunque became propaganda boss for the Reds and since any occasion offered him a pretext for starting a discussion, it wasn't long before everyone understood what he was up to and avoided getting into one with him. Everyone, that is, except the Reds themselves, for whom Comunque was a paragon of logical rigour, that inflexible logic against which no objection can be made by any opponent who is left standing. And the Reds, of course, were the only people interested in Comunque and the Party.

*

Don Camillo was not a fussy eater, but he couldn't swallow this damned Comunque. Peppone, on the other hand, had no choice but to do so, because the first time he got into a discussion with Comunque at the Party HQ over a disagreement about some of his statements, Comunque said to him:

'Comrade, your objections are the classic ones that a reactionary would make. Do I have to answer you as if you were a reactionary, or is it enough to remind you that what I have just set out is the Party's point of view?'

'The Party's point of view, if I am not mistaken,' replied Peppone, 'is that democratic discussion is permitted within the Party.'

'Democratic discussion is permitted, but not using anti-democratic arguments,' asserted Comunque.

Peppone thought it best not to continue the discussion because he knew very well that it would be hard to construe a kick up Comunque's backside as a democratic argument. He swallowed hard and ended the debate.

Nevertheless, the next time he met Don Camillo, he showed himself far from dissatisfied with Comunque's work. 'Unless I'm much mistaken, Father, I reckon we've got just the chap to put an end to your pedagogy' he exclaimed. 'It's no easy task to outwit the young man!'

'Impossible,' replied Don Camillo calmly. 'But the Party School managed it.'

'It's easy to joke your way out of trouble,' retorted Peppone. 'Not so easy to get the better of my young man.'

'If not impossible. Ask him what's two plus two, and he answers, "Tomorrow's Friday."'

'Comunque,' Peppone sneered . . . 'Seems to be working so far.'

'Have you learned to say "Comunque" as well?' enquired Don Camillo. 'Is communism now Comunque-ism?'

'Father, it seems to me that when you too are asked what's two plus two, you answer "Tomorrow's Friday."'

'That may be so, but with the simple difference that I say it on Thursday, whereas your champion says it on Tuesday and Saturday.'

'I'd like to see you prove that!' exclaimed Peppone.

'Impossible, comrade Mayor. Your party's calendar bears no relation to the calendar of decent people.'

Peppone went on the attack. 'Father, doesn't it stick in your craw that you put on such a miserable show on the one occasion you tried to shut Cesarino up?'

'That may be so. But you have never managed it either.'

This stung Peppone. 'What's that got to do with it?'

'It's got everything to do with it, because I don't understand how you can still be head of your Section when there's somebody in it who reasons better than you do.'

'There's a lot of things you don't understand! I can tell you this, Comunque . . .'

'Are we Comunque-ing again?' interrupted Don Camillo with a mischievous smile.

'Go to hell, you and your pronouns!' shouted Peppone, turning his back and marching off in fury . . .

*

After a year of intense oratorical activity, Comunque was recalled to the city to have the jukebox retuned and its repertoire updated. He returned perfectly lubricated and with a complete set of new recordings wholly dedicated to Russia: Russia's extraordinary progress, Russia's firm desire for peace, the necessity of loving Russia even if it meant hating all the other peoples of the world, the urgent need to denounce the North Atlantic Treaty in order to secure important commercial relationships and cultural exchanges with Russia, and so on. Comunque hurled himself into the Sovietisation of the masses and fired off breathtaking oratorical salvoes. Then, just as he reached the peak of his exaltation, it happened . . . The *carabinieri* sent for Comunque on an urgent personal matter, and off he went.

He reappeared in front of Peppone late in the evening, and with a gloomy look on his face.

'What did they want?' asked Peppone anxiously.

'I'm in serious trouble,' answered Comunque. 'Get rid of the others. It's a very delicate matter.'

Once they were alone in the People's Palace, Peppone turned to Comunque: 'Right then, out with it!'

Comunque spread his arms: 'Boss, it's a personal matter, but seeing how busy I am at the moment, it could, in a way, end up damaging the Party.'

'Don't mess me about! What have you been getting up to?'

'Nothing, it's an old story. You know how I had to fight in the war, like a load of others. And I had to fight people I didn't know, and I had to serve the wrong cause and become the tool of dictators' violence. And I was part of that betrayed generation who opened their eyes too late, and I, like so many others, unconsciously served the interests of arms dealers and tyrants . . .'

'Enough of that,' Peppone interrupted him. 'I'm not asking for a self-denunciation. This is all on your Party record. You were a corporal in Supplies in Greece.'

Comunque shook his head. 'That's what it says in the record, but I wasn't actually in Supplies in Greece. I fought as a rifleman in Russia . . .'

Peppone looked up sharply. 'You've acted like a total idiot. You should have told the truth. This is the sort of thing kids and women get up to. Anyway, I don't see what the fuss is about. How do the *carabinieri* come into it? What shady business did you get up to in Russia?'

'This,' whispered Comunque, handing Peppone a fat scroll. 'The *carabinieri* delivered this to me yesterday.'

Peppone spread the scroll across his desk. It was a decree awarding a silver medal for military valour to Rifleman Corporal Cesare Delfosso: and the citation was long and significant. Peppone read the decree carefully and then looked up.

'Voluntary?' he asked darkly.

'Yes,' replied the humiliated Comunque.

'Promoted to Corporal for daring deeds of war!'

'Yes.'

'So . . . alone, with hand grenades you went to flush out and eliminate three Russian soldiers who had been machine-gunning a crossing point inflicting grave losses on the advancing Italian units!'

Comunque flung out his arms. 'When I saw my best friend, Gigi, mown down beside me, I lost control.'

'And when you did . . . the other exploit that got you awarded the corporal's stripes?'

'The heat of battle . . . We were all a bit crazy . . .'

'And how hot were you when you volunteered for the expeditionary force against Russia?'

'I don't know, I was so young . . . They'd poisoned our minds at school . . . I belong to that unhappy generation . . .'

'You've explained all that already! Now try explaining how I'm supposed to come to your rescue when you're telling a meeting about our Russian brothers etcetera, and that damned Don Camillo waves a newspaper under our noses with an article about your silver medal and the citation and all the rest of it.'

'No newspaper's going to print that!' protested Comunque.

'If Don Camillo wasn't the paper's main source of rural news, and if he wasn't a man who sticks his nose into everything, I might be able to get you out of this. But seeing how things are, it's 10,000 lire to a button that the day after tomorrow there'll be three columns about you in the paper. So how am I going to get you out of that?'

Comunque gnashed his teeth and remained lost in thought for some time, but to no avail. Then Peppone came to his aid.

'There is just one solution. As soon as they wave the newspaper under your nose, you reply, "This is no surprise, I expected it. In fact, here's the decree." You pull the decree out of your pocket, then you tear it into a thousand pieces and declare "I wholeheartedly reject this medal, which reminds me of a shameful past that I disown. I was mistaken, as a hundred thousand other young men of my age were mistaken, victims of dictatorship's criminal propaganda. And in the face of dictatorship, and in your faces too, I throw the scraps of this shameful past that will never come again . . ." Etcetera. Prepare your little speech and then, tomorrow morning, come and let me hear it so that we can go over the details.'

'Right you are, boss,' said Comunque, as he put his scroll back in his pocket and left. 'I'll make those damned bourgeois enemies of the people drop dead from rage.'

*

Peppone had not been wrong. At that moment, Don Camillo was walking up and down the presbytery, in the grip of the utmost agitation. He already knew the whole story. They had brought him a complete copy of the decree and a photo, the photo of a small group of riflemen cheerfully showing a poster on which they had written:

> *When we're in Moscow we'll hold a fair,*
> *and show those Bolshies that we're at home there.*

And in the front row, holding the poster in his very own hands, was Rifleman Cesarino Delfosso, aka Comunque.

Don Camillo couldn't calm himself sufficiently to sit down at the table and draft the article to send to the newspaper. Besides, he was in a state of uncertainty: should he send the photo and article to the paper or print some notices to distribute during Comunque's next political meeting?

At last he sat down and picked up his pen: he had decided on the newspaper. He dipped the pen in ink, tried it out on a piece of scrap paper, and when he was sure it was working perfectly, flung it away. The nib stuck in the side of a chest of drawers and stayed there, together with all the temptations Don Camillo had overcome.

*

Next morning, Comunque came to visit Peppone.

'Have you prepared your little speech?' asked Peppone gruffly.

'Yes,' replied Comunque.

'Let's hear it.'

Comunque stood with his head bowed for a few moments as if to meditate upon the words he had assembled. Then he said, 'You can wave all the newspapers you like. I won't tear anything up. I earned that medal and I'm keeping it.'

Peppone shook his great head very slightly. 'Do you realise exactly what you're saying?'

'Yes. I've been thinking it over all night. I cannot feel ashamed of having been a good soldier. Back then I was convinced that I was serving my country and, to me, the Russians I was fighting were my country's enemies.'

Peppone looked at him sternly. 'And aren't you ashamed, now that your eyes are opened and you know how things were and are, aren't you ashamed of having done away with three poor fellows who were defending their invaded country?'

'I'm sorry, but I cannot feel ashamed,' explained Comunque.

'This is very serious.'

'It would be worse if I should boast of being a deserter.'

'If you'd been a deserter, you wouldn't be feeling guilty today for having actively participated in an unjust war.'

'You only know if a war is just or unjust when it's over. If you lose it's unjust, if you win it's just. Back then I only knew it was my duty to go and fight like the others.'

'Good,' concluded Peppone. 'If you had come to tell me that you were agreeing to tear up your medal award I'd have kicked you straight out of here.'

'No danger of that. I'd sooner tear up my Party card than tear up that piece of paper.'

'Don't worry, you can keep them both,' Peppone reassured him. 'I'll see to it that all this gets sorted out.'

As soon as he was inside the presbytery, Peppone laid all his cards on the table. 'Father, in case you don't know this already, I'm informing you that the so-called "Comunque", the one who nowadays speaks publicly in favour of Russia, accepted a silver medal for a heroic feat of arms performed in combat *against* the Russians.'

'I knew that already,' replied Don Camillo.

'I thought you would. So I am certain that, if you haven't already done so, you'll be preparing to give this information to the newspaper in such a way as to cause embarrassment to the said Comunque.'

'On the contrary,' replied Don Camillo. 'The internal affairs of your party are of no interest to me.'

Peppone turned red with rage. 'As I understand it, Father, it is only when dishonourable things happen to my party that they are of any interest to you. If one of my men is praised for being a good soldier, this doesn't interest you. It's a strange way of being a correspondent for the so-called "independent newspaper". If you were an honest man, you'd put the good things in as well as the bad ones.'

Don Camillo stood up, went to the corner of his closet, pulled the pen out of the wood, straightened the nib, and sitting at the table, dashed off a few lines: '*In recognition of a heroic act of war during the course of which he succeeded, alone, in reaching and destroying a machine-gun placement stoutly held by three enemy soldiers, the Silver Medal for Military Valour has been awarded to Rifleman Corporal Cesare Delfosso.*'

He showed the paper to Peppone who read the notice carefully, and finally commented, 'If it had been one of yours, you'd have made a novel out of it!'

Don Camillo spread his arms and solemnly pronounced, 'If God gives you a finger, don't take his whole hand.'

'I didn't know they'd promoted you to the rank of Almighty,' remarked Peppone. 'Do you want me to pay you now for your trouble, or should I wait for you to send the bill to my home address?'

'Wait for the bill. But I won't be sending it. The Almighty will send it to you when the time is right.'

'I hope you'll be so good as to get me a discount,' said Peppone, and he went home well satisfied.

L'Étranger

No one in the area had ever seen as many foreigners as there were that summer. They came from everywhere and in every kind of vehicle. Quite a few even came with no vehicle at all, *pedibus calcantibus*, but with a bit of patience and a lot of cheek they still managed to travel through half of Italy, thumbing lifts.

Naturally the foreign hitchhikers only worked the busy main roads, so when one of these characters turned up on the dreariest little side road in the whole of the Lower Plain, it was extraordinary enough to leave everyone scratching their heads.

Peppone nearly ran into this chap at the end of the Crociletto road when, taken by surprise, he slammed on the brakes, stopped his truck just in time, and made Smilzo smack his head against the windscreen. Peppone then muttered an oath or two, opened the window and yelled in fury, 'What do you think you're playing at?'

The man stammered something incomprehensible and Peppone started to calm down, while considering the stranger with penetrating curiosity. He was a podgy little chap in his forties with straw-coloured hair, wearing knee-length shorts, a sleeveless vest, sandals and a kind of beret. On his shoulders he carried a well-stuffed rucksack.

'Foreign type,' said Smilzo, still rubbing his forehead. 'Must be one of those tourists.'

The little man came up to the window and smiled.

'*Excusez* me . . . If you can *prendre* me *sur votre* car . . . I toward Rome . . .'

Peppone burst out laughing and replied:

'Nix Rome! We go little town! Rome need Via Emilia and then Bologna. You about-turn and forward-march! Got it?'

With much difficulty and in the most comical Italian ever heard, the little man explained that he hadn't yet learned to speak Italian, but he could understand it. 'Please to speak own language. Quite slow, please.'

Peppone explained, in words and gestures, that he was terribly off-track, and told him how he could get to Via Emilia. Helped by Smilzo, he sketched a map on a piece of paper and wrote the number of kilometres: 35.

The little man put his face over his hands in dismay. '*Trente-cinq kilomètres*!' he exclaimed. 'That truckiste *méchant* who take me at Piacenza and put me down here say, "*Vingt-cinq minutes et puis Bologne*!"' Since it was getting late he asked if he could at least be taken to a town where he might find somewhere to sleep. Peppone told the man to jump in, and off they went.

'Where are you from?' he asked as they drove along.

'Paris. I French,' answered the little man.

Peppone whistled in amazement. 'You're going all the way from Paris to Rome!' he exclaimed, 'and travelling like this all the way?'

'*Oui monsieur.*'

'That's crazy!' said Peppone. 'How can you possibly travel like that?'

The little man shrugged. '*Pour voyager il faut de l'argent, beaucoup d'argent! Je n'ai pas d'argent!* I small money and so I make travel small-money way.'

Peppone snorted. '*Balle!* You could stay at home for nothing!'

The little man sighed and gave a melancholy smile.

'All the *année travailler, toujours travailler*, and so need some days to go away . . . See beautiful things . . . New things . . . *Compris, monsieur?*'

Peppone had understood perfectly, and shook his head. He changed the subject.

'So, how do you like Italy?'

'*Formidable!*' exclaimed the little man. '*Formidable!*'

Peppone found this highly flattering and continued his enquiry: 'And our region, Emilia, what do you think of it?'

The man shrugged again.

'Don't you understand?' Peppone went on. 'I asked how you like Emilia?'

The man seemed embarrassed.

'Understand. Emilia very beautiful . . . Much agriculture . . . Good food . . .' Clearly the little man found something amiss with Emilia but didn't dare say so.

'Speak freely!' exclaimed Peppone. 'What is it you don't like?'

'I like all!' cried the man. 'But I much fear.'

Peppone stopped the truck and turned to him. 'You're afraid? Why's that?'

'Please, sir,' stammered the man, getting into quite a state. 'I not offend. Emilia most very beautiful, but I fear of politic. I do no politic, sir. I only *travailler*.'

'What harm has been done to you in Emilia?' he yelled.

'Nothing, monsieur. No bad thing! Only very good, very kind and friendly *tout le monde* . . . But I hear say, I read newspaper, much terrible *politique* in Emilia. . . . All communist in Emilia, and when you are not communist, *tuer!*'

'Tew-ay?' asked Peppone. 'What's tew-ay?'

'Bam! Bam!' replied the Frenchman, imitating the firing of a rifle. '*Les communistes* of Emilia bam bam *tous les prêtres*, all priests, burn churches . . . Much terrible, frighten.'

Peppone turned to Smilzo. 'Hear that?' he growled. 'Hear what people abroad think about us, because of what our reactionary swine are writing in the papers? See how terrified this poor wretch is? He can't wait to get out of here! He thinks he's ended up in a den of murderers.'

Smilzo spread his arms. 'But what can we do about it, boss? If that's what they think, we can't change it.'

'Oh yes we can!' replied Peppone. 'You watch how I handle this little dope! He'll have a completely different opinion when he goes home!'

Peppone had spoken in rapid dialect, so the Frenchman hadn't understood a word and his eyes were big with apprehension. Peppone turned to him and said, 'See this red thing on the lapel of my jacket? Well, it's the badge of the Communist Party! I communist, my comrade here communist! I boss of all the communists!'

He pulled his Party card out of his wallet and shoved it under the Frenchman's nose. 'Understood?'

The poor little man was terrified. 'Please, sir,' he stammered. 'I get down . . . much thanks . . . *Merci bien* . . . I not offend . . . I not politic . . . I no party . . . I only *travailler* . . . I two children and wife . . . please no hurt . . .'

Peppone started the truck: 'Don't be afraid,' he reassured him. 'You have been misinformed. All false reactionary propaganda. I will show you the truth.'

The Frenchman did not really seem convinced, and shortly afterwards, seeing a priest on a bicycle appear on the road, he turned pale. Peppone noticed this and winked at Smilzo. When the truck and the bicycle were about to pass each other, Peppone stopped and got out. When the priest was a few steps away, Peppone took off his hat, made a slight bow, took a piece of paper from his pocket and held it out to the priest, who stopped and got off his bike.

'What on earth has come over you, comrade Mayor?' asked Don Camillo grimly.

'Nothing Father,' replied Peppone with an angelic smile. 'I would be grateful if, at a convenient moment, you could take a look at this note. Good evening.'

And with a great flourish of his hat, he took his leave, got back into the cab and set off, leaving Don Camillo staring after them.

'Life has been hard,' explained Peppone to the Frenchman with a sigh, 'ever since the priests took over in Emilia. If you need to travel anywhere by truck you have to show a permit. They check everything. They check everything for the government.'

The Frenchman's eyes were bulging. '*Mais c'est incroyable*!' he stammered.

'You don't know how incredible!' sighed Peppone.

When they arrived, Peppone drove straight to the People's Palace. 'This is our headquarters, the HQ of the Communist Party,' Peppone explained to the Frenchman. 'Come in and make yourself at home. There's a nice bedroom on the first floor. Be our guest.'

The Frenchman didn't have a clue what was going on, and allowed himself to be led upstairs.

'Arrange things as you please,' said Peppone, introducing him to the room. 'The wash basin is in the little room there on the left. Make yourself comfortable, and I'll come for you in an hour or so.'

An hour later, Peppone knocked on the door. The Frenchman had given himself a shave and tidied himself up as best he could.

'Leave your bag, by all means,' Peppone told him. 'It's perfectly safe here. Let's go down.'

The assembly room was full of people. Smilzo had done a good job.

'Comrades,' said Peppone, 'we have here an honoured foreign guest, a French worker, to whom I am glad to extend a hearty welcome!'

There was a round of applause which turned the little man pale. They all came to shake his hand and everyone smiled at him. Then at a sign from Peppone, they all fell silent and arranged themselves in an orderly row in front of the stage.

'Are you a Catholic?' Peppone asked the Frenchman.

'*Oh, oui!*'

'Then you can stay,' Peppone reassured him.

A bell rang and everyone stood to attention. The curtain opened to reveal a Crucifix, enthroned above a little altar that was decked out in white, red and green. Peppone started reciting the Lord's Prayer and everyone joined in. Then a Hail Mary. At the end they all crossed themselves and the curtain closed.

'We have to do this,' explained Peppone to the Frenchman. 'The priests want to turn local Catholics against us, so they've excommunicated us and banned us from entering the church. And we, who are all sincere, practising Catholics, have to say our prayers in secret. But God knows, and will justly punish those who merit it.'

The Frenchman's eyes were full of tears, and he kept on murmuring, '*C'est incroyable!*'

They had dinner at Peppone's house, and all his top brass were there.

'I'm sorry I can only offer you eggs, fish and vegetable soup, but today being Friday, if the ecclesiastical authorities knew we weren't eating plainly they'd have us arrested. They are implacable!' exclaimed Peppone.

'*C'est incroyable!*' murmured the Frenchman again.

It was a thoroughly cheerful and tranquil meal. Towards nine o'clock, Peppone's children all came to give their dad a kiss on his forehead, even the eldest, who was about to be called up. 'Don't forget your prayers!' warned Peppone as the clutch of children left the room.

They discussed local matters, and what an extraordinary discussion it was, one fit for inclusion in a manual on democracy. Smilzo spoke about the farmworkers' strike: 'The comrades voted unanimously against! Nobody wants to strike because it would severely damage the harvest. If the clergy want a strike for political reasons, to show America that the communist threat is alive and real, we will oppose it democratically, but firmly. We shall work!'

'Hear hear!' responded the others. When it was nearly midnight, after some rousing rustic choruses, the meeting closed and the Frenchman made his way back to the People's Palace.

'It is a wonderful thing!' exclaimed the Frenchman. 'It is terrible how the propaganda paint the contrary. I finally comprehend the situation of Emilia, this *région* extraordinary of agriculture and *generosité*. When I shall return to Paris I will say the truth. Thank you. *Merci bien!*'

The Frenchman slept the deepest sleep of his life, and next morning, when he came downstairs with his rucksack on his back, he found breakfast already prepared. And outside, the side-car was waiting for him.

'The boss has ordered me to take you to your next stop,' explained Smilzo.

The Frenchman got into the side-car and had tears in his eyes as they left the little town. Smilzo headed off like a rocket, but stopped after only three kilometres.

'Here's the station,' he explained. 'The communist workers here don't want you to exhaust yourself by travelling on foot. Take the train. Good luck, comrade!'

Smilzo handed the Frenchman an envelope, remounted his motorbike, and set off like a lightning bolt.

'*C'est incroyable!*' stammered the Frenchman, and turned towards the station, but took no more than two steps before he found someone standing in his way. It was Don Camillo. He had followed Smilzo on his own motorbike, slipping into a side road whenever Smilzo stopped, and waiting till he could safely set off again.

'*Bonjour,*' said Don Camillo with a smile. 'I heard that you had been a guest at the People's Palace and, before you go, I would like to make sure that they have treated you with every respect.'

'*Formidable!* Excellent!' replied the Frenchman with enthusiasm. 'Many fine gentlemen. *Je suis très heureux de les avoir connus!* I had fear of the communists when I arrive, *mais* I not fear more. All bad propaganda. I permit myself, *monsieur l'archiprête, de vous dire que aujourd'hui* I think I am more fear of the clergy.'

'I would be grateful for a little chat with you,' said Don Camillo. 'We will have lunch together in that restaurant over there. We will be tranquil and you will eat well.'

Don Camillo waited until the Frenchman was fully re-fuelled before saying what was on his mind, and seeing the man become more expansive and talkative once he was full of food and wine, he launched the subject of his stay in the town. It didn't take much to get the little man going. The Frenchman told him in minute detail what had happened, concluding with his belief that he had never found kinder, more generous, religious,

democratic, gentle people than these, exclaiming yet
again, '*C'est incroyable!*'

'They've toyed with you like a child!' retorted Don
Camillo. 'They've put on a disgraceful comic charade
and are now laughing at you behind your back!'

The Frenchman's eyes widened. 'I not understand . . .
I see with my eyes . . .'

Don Camillo shook his head. 'You don't know their
methods! You are fooling yourself that they are really the
way you saw them. Oh, you naïve man!'

Don Camillo talked and talked with vehemence, in
Italian, in French, in Latin, with his eyes and with his
hands, and the little man listened, becoming more and
more disturbed every minute. Finally, he covered his face
with his hands.

'*C'est terrible!*' he exclaimed in anguish. 'I never
imagine the human *perfidie* reach such *limite*! *C'est épou-
vantable!* I wish to be tomorrow at Rome and to kneel
before St Peter and ask God pardon of the sin of these
criminal! I wish to be now in the Holy City to purify me.
And then to Paris! See again my home and my young
ones.'

Don Camillo consoled the poor little man, explaining
to him that even the Devil is not as bad as he is painted.
There are two sides to every question. Yes, they pulled
the wool over his eyes, but that didn't make them criminals, just people who have taken the wrong road and can
be brought back from it. That's all. He shouldn't go
away with a mistaken impression. What was being said
and written in France about Emilia was false, a denigra-
tion. The men who deceived him had indeed behaved in
a most reprehensible manner, but they weren't bandits or
wolves in sheep's clothing. Why not be Don Camillo's
guest for a couple of days, so as to understand how things
really were?

The Frenchman shook his head. '*C'est impossible!*' How could he go back to the town? They would recognise him, and who knows what they might get up to if they saw him being a guest of the priest?

'Don't worry,' Don Camillo reassured him. 'I'll find you a suit and hat and some sunglasses. Nobody will recognise you. You have to do this: it's important that you go home with the right idea about our region. Nothing is clear when you're sitting at a table in a restaurant.'

*

Once he had been made respectable-looking, the Frenchman bore not the slightest resemblance to the down-at-heel hitchhiker of a few days earlier. He was a likeable man and kept Don Camillo company for almost a week. He took note of the true situation in Emilia and the character of its people. When he left, Don Camillo would not permit him to go back into his back-packer's rags, which he put into a suitcase, and gave him the money for his journey to Rome. Then Don Camillo took him to the station on his motorbike. He went onto the platform with him, helped him aboard, and waited for the train to leave.

When the whistle blew, the Frenchman stuck his head out of the window and said to Don Camillo, '*Au revoir Monseigneur* . . . I'm not from Paris. I'm from Naples . . . I've travelled all round Italy, pretending to be a foreign hitchhiker, and now I'm going home. . . There's still time for me to get off the train and go with you to the *carabinieri*.'

Don Camillo sighed. '*Bon voyage* . . . When a man is as on the ball as you are, I'd rather he was an Italian than a foreigner. *Au revoir Monsieur!*'

'*Au revoir Monseigneur! . . .*'

Smortíno

'WHAT'S NEW?' ASKED Peppone on the way into his office at the People's Palace.

Lungo rose to his feet, went over to close the door, took a letter from his pocket and handed it without a word to Peppone. It was from Smortíno, one of the gang's smartest operators, and contained his resignation from the Party. In a couple of lines he explained that he could no longer reconcile his duty as a Catholic with that of being a militant Communist.

The papers that morning had carried the news of an activist from Bologna who had just left the Party, as a communist MP from the south had done only a few weeks earlier, and Peppone had been in a foul mood all day. Now, after a heavy dinner, there was Smortíno's letter to give him indigestion.

'What's going on!' he exclaimed.

'Nothing is going on,' answered Lungo. 'Weak suggestive characters have succumbed to subversive propaganda. They read the news trumpeted by the newspapers and get into a state about it. It's the same story with people who kill themselves. Nothing to worry about.'

Peppone banged a fist on his desk. 'Oh, I see! We have to stay calm and stand by while even this sort of news is printed by the newspapers, so that other weak characters can read it and get into a state and leave the Party.'

Lungo shook his head. 'No, we must instead make sure that this kind of thing is not printed in the newspapers. Smortíno brought his letter here ten minutes ago and then slipped away. We should send for him and talk . . . nicely to him. Find out how things stand, see if anybody else knows about his decision. Make him see sense and everything will be fine.'

Just then Smilzo arrived on the scene and they told him to go and fetch Smortíno because they needed to talk to him, and Smilzo jumped on his bike and shot off. A little while later he was back, explaining that Smortíno wasn't at home, and his mother didn't know where he was either.

'That's not good!' muttered Lungo. 'Either he's hiding at home and his mother's in on it, or he's hiding somewhere else and she isn't . . . Let's go see.'

The thing had to be handled with a certain grace and perspicacity, a particular challenge to Peppone's lot but one greatly facilitated by the fact that the house where Smortíno lived with his mother was secluded and some way out of the village.

'One of us should lie in wait beside the embankment, one by the road, and one by the vegetable garden,' proposed Lungo. 'If he's at home, amen. If he's out, he'll come back, and unless he drops down from the sky, we'll get him for sure.'

They prepared the ground for the expedition with great care. The three of them went and had a drink at the café in the piazza's arcade, and made a show of chatting with the people around them. Then Smilzo announced that he was feeling sleepy and was going to bed. After he left, Lungo declared to the assembled throng that he too was tired and went home. It was another quarter of an hour before Peppone started yawning and also wished the gang goodnight, making his way through the mist to his home base. Once there, he went in through the front door before making his way stealthily out the back door, crossing the fields to reach the place they'd chosen for the stake-out. Smilzo and Lungo were, of course, already in position in their two sectors.

It was a murky and very cold night, but the three allies had thick hides and, when one o'clock sounded, they were still to be found in position as silent and immobile as stones. Smortíno arrived a little later on the embankment side of the house, and it was Peppone who took hold of him.

'We want a word or two with you,' he said in a low voice, and gave a short whistle whereupon the other two joined them. Smortíno offered no resistance and walked without a word alongside the expeditionary force of three. He got a bit worried when he realised that, instead of making for the road, Peppone and company were leading him into the middle of the fields, so deeply shrouded in mist.

'Where are you taking me?' he asked.

'Somewhere quiet for a chat,' answered Lungo. And they couldn't have chosen anywhere more quiet than Castorta, an abandoned property lost to scrub, where no living soul ever ventured. When they arrived they managed to generate enough light to find their way into that nest of bats and ghosts. Beyond a door, bolted and padlocked, lay a large hall with a vaulted ceiling and bricked-up windows, which had once served as a wine cellar and was still in good condition – it had later been used by tenant farmers on the local estate to store unwanted odds and ends. Peppone easily opened the rusty lock with a nail, and the gang took possession of the room. Lying around, both inside and out, were a number of posts, joists and half rotten tables, and so a lively fire was soon cheering that frozen den of darkness.

Peppone warmed himself in silence for a few minutes and then observed with satisfaction: 'We can talk in peace here because even if the four of us started screaming like crazy, God Almighty himself wouldn't hear us.'

Smortíno got the message, but deliberately showed no reaction.

'Smortíno,' Peppone resumed after a while, 'I have received a letter that I would rather not have received. Did writing it cause you . . . a little unease by any chance?'

'Yes,' replied Smortíno, 'I was sorry that I had to write it, especially to you. But what's done is done.'

'That is not so,' objected Peppone. 'What is done can also be undone. Especially when it was done at a time of . . . mental imbalance.'

Smortíno shook his head. 'I wrote it with a completely clear head,' he replied. 'I've been thinking about it for years.'

'Oh, indeed! Since when, exactly?' Peppone sneered.

'Since the night you, Smilzo, Lungo and me found ourselves surrounded by Germans machine-gunning us at Castellina. I thought I was done for, and I prayed to God. And he saved me.'

'What about Peppone, Smilzo and me?' exclaimed Lungo. 'How come we were saved too, yet we didn't pray to God?'

'Only you can know the answer to that,' replied Smortíno. 'Anyway, the issue is not the fact that God saved me. I know what I felt inside when I turned to God: I felt that even if they killed me, I was not lost. It's hard to explain . . .'

'It's not so hard to understand, though,' responded Lungo. 'What is less easy is how your belief in God has anything to do with your resignation from the Party. Does the Party forbid you to believe in God?'

'No,' responded Smortíno calmly, 'but God forbids me to believe in the Party.'

Lungo leaped to his feet. 'Not God! – the priest! Not God, but the slut who's turned your head and yet won't have you because you're a political opponent of her father's false Democrazia Cristiana party. We know all about it . . .'

'You know nothing about it,' Smortíno answered, again calmly. 'This has got nothing to do with priests or girls. It has to do with my conscience.'

Peppone intervened. 'Smortíno,' he said sharply, 'do you have any idea of the harm you're doing to the Communist party by your decision? Do you have any idea of the rotten speculation that our opponents will stir up around what you've done? Aren't you ashamed to think about what the newspapers of the enemies of the people will write about you?'

Smortíno spread his arms. 'I have resigned, you will take my name off the register, and that's that. There's no call for anyone to go spreading the story all over the place.'

'Idiot!' shouted Lungo. 'You aren't just *any* comrade. You're a leader, one of the inner circle. We'll have to expel you as a traitor, and you'll have to defend yourself by telling the whole story.'

Smortíno was incredulous. 'And why do you want to expel me as a traitor? I haven't betrayed anyone.'

Lungo cut him short. 'Enough! We didn't come here to waste time in useless discussion. We've explained to you how things are and what it boils down to is this: we are living at a special moment in time, and we cannot afford any more scandal. Withdraw your letter and we'll say no more about it.'

'No,' responded Smortíno. 'I *cannot* withdraw it.'

Lungo looked him in the eye. 'Why not?' he asked menacingly. 'Perhaps you have already blabbed about this?'

'No, I haven't told anyone.'

'No one at all? Not even your . . . mother?'

At this, Smortíno somehow managed to turn even paler.

'What's my mother got to do with it? It's nobody's business but mine!'

'So much the better,' chuckled Lungo. 'It's just as well your mother has nothing to do with it, and that she knows nothing about letters and no-letters. That way the matter remains between us. Smortíno, if you won't withdraw your letter, you have another way out. You get a piece of paper, you write on it that you beg forgiveness for what you are doing, but that you can't live without the woman you love, and that her family won't let you have her for political reasons. Then you take this rope, tie it to that hook on the ceiling there and hang yourself.'

Smortíno started laughing.

'Lungo, I'm not in the mood for jokes.'

Lungo jumped to his feet. 'Neither are we!' he yelled in fury.

Smortíno took a step backwards, but fell into Peppone's arms, where he found himself gripped as if in a vice. At a sign from Lungo, Smilzo dived and took hold of Smortíno's legs.

'Now look at you. A dried codfish!' sneered Lungo. 'With the difference that the codfish has no head, but you've still got yours, which is very handy for us.'

Lungo was nifty with his hands and, snatching up the thick rope lying at his feet, he improvised a noose of the highest quality. 'Smortíno,' he explained fiercely, 'everyone, even the cats, knows about your love-sick sufferings of the heart. Tomorrow, when they find you hanged, they'll all say, "Poor Smortíno, driven mad by unrequited love." That's it in a nutshell. Now I pull the noose tight, then we hang you from the hook, and move that overturned chest near to your feet. You're wearing your overcoat and a cloak over that. No trace of violence, even though Peppone is holding tightly onto your arms. A foggy night. Nobody saw you come, and nobody will see you leave. All perfect.'

Smortíno knew Lungo, and gave himself up for lost. Lost as he had been at Castellina.

'Smortíno, decide before I count to three,' said Lungo darkly, 'either you withdraw the letter or I throttle you! Will you withdraw it? One . . . two . . .'

'No,' answered Smortíno. 'I fear God more than I fear you.'

Lungo flexed his muscles and started to tighten the noose. Then threw down the rope. 'It's not worth the trouble, dirtying our hands on a worm like you,' he said.

Peppone and Smilzo let Smortíno go and went to sit by the fire.

'The trial is over,' announced Lungo. 'You're acquitted of the charge of betrayal by reason of mental infirmity. But you're still liable for costs!'

Rage was taking hold of Lungo again and, picking up a stave from the floor, he advanced towards Smortíno with the clear intention of using it to break his back.

'You'll pay the costs of the trial!' he yelled, raising the stick.

'The costs of the trial,' said a voice, 'will be paid by Stalin.'

And since the voice gave every indication of coming out of a gleaming iron barrel that Don Camillo was holding tightly between his hands, Lungo dropped his stick.

*

Don Camillo advanced cautiously and, after taking a good look at Smortíno, who was still lying there like a dried codfish, with the rope around his neck, he chuckled: 'A tie with a "Prague" style knot! . . . Come on, take off that necklace and go home while I have a little chat with these fine fellows.'

Smortíno took off the noose and left without a word. Then Don Camillo went and sat down in the doorway.

'So that piece of scum had planned this little game with you all along!' bellowed Peppone.

'No,' responded Don Camillo calmly. 'He didn't plan anything with anyone. But his mother knew he had sent the letter, and when she saw Smilzo arriving to call her son to the People's Palace, she got worried and ran to me for advice . . . Which was to go to bed, while I went to take a little look at what was going on. So, I watched your manoeuvres at the café. And when you jumped Smortíno, the poor archpriest was there, four steps behind you. And he followed you here. And waited patiently, in hiding, behind the door.'

Lungo started to speak but got no further than, 'You . . .'

'Shut up, Executioner!' exclaimed Don Camillo brandishing menacingly his burnished weapon.

'You frighten me enough when you brandish a candelabra!' cried Peppone, stepping forward. 'But I'll tell you this: there is no more treacherous an individual in the entire universe than you!'

Don Camillo shook his head. 'No, Comrade Peppone. If I were the most treacherous individual in the universe, then instead of coming in when Lungo picked up the stick, I would have come in at the moment when you two were holding Smortíno down while Lungo tightened the noose. And in that scenario, how would you ever have convinced me that your intention was not to strangle Smortíno, but just to scare him?'

Don Camillo took an ember from the fire and lit his half Tuscan. 'I'm not your unscrupulous traffic cop on the lookout in a no-parking area, waiting until the driver leaves before slipping a ticket under his windscreen wiper. I am not preying on the situation here, I'm your honest cop who, when he sees a driver stopping in a prohibited place, tells him, "You can't park here. Try somewhere else."'

Peppone grumbled that this had nothing to do with it. Indeed what happened was the exact opposite . . .

'By no means, brother. It is not the opposite, because after seeing you snatch that poor creature and bring him here, if I had intervened straight away, no one would ever have been able to remove the suspicion etched on their mind that you intended to do away with Smortíno. I wanted to be sure how far you might go, and when I saw you pulling on that noose, I refused to believe you were that kind of scum. I had faith in you and now I am happy because my mission is not that of a police patrolman who has to give the commissioner a nightly list of twenty or thirty or fifty people stopped and searched and locked up as suspected criminals, even when they are actually perfectly respectable gentlemen who have gone out for a moment to buy some cigarettes, but left their wallets and ID at home. No, I am the pastor who goes out at night to find the lost sheep and bring it back to the fold. Not the shepherd who goes out at night to see if wolves are roaming around the sheepfold and if he sees the lost sheep says, "You are a wolf, because only wolves go out at night while sheep spend their nights in the fold," and then treats the sheep like a wolf and shoots it.'

Peppone snorted, 'Save your sermons for Smortíno!'

'He doesn't need them. He found his own way back to the fold.'

'I wish you joy with him! The trouble we've had, getting rid of him! We've freed ourselves of a cell of the enemy!'

Don Camillo shrugged. 'One? What's one in all the hundreds of thousands of enemy cells lurking among you?'

Peppone started to laugh. 'If it comes to that, we can always sleep with an extra pillow, Father!'

'Sleep, Peppone, but while you're sleeping the cell is at work.' Don Camillo touched Peppone's ample chest with his index finger. 'The enemy cell is hidden *in there*. It's called your conscience.'

Smilzo changed the subject. 'Just think how we'll laugh, seeing Smortíno dressed like a daughter of Mary with a ribbon round his neck!'

Don Camillo shook his head.

'*Mah!* When I saw Smortíno with the noose around his neck insisting, "I won't withdraw anything", it didn't make me want to laugh. If I'm not mistaken, Smortíno is a young man with his head very much screwed on.'

'Glad to hear it!' exclaimed Peppone proudly. 'He graduated from my school! All my graduates have their heads screwed on!'

The other two – also hatched in Peppone's hen-house – puffed out their chests with pride.

'The Old Guard dies but never surrenders!' Smilzo chimed in like the Voice of History.

Don Camillo looked at him curiously. 'Does not surrender to whom?'

'To whoever it may be!' cried Lungo.

'To *whom*ever *you* may be,' added Peppone solemnly, as if to make it clear to Don Camillo that the Old Guard feared no attacks at all, whether in the third person nomi-native or the second person dative.

In the face of so massive a resistance, Don Camillo lifted the siege and withdrew.

The Joke

WHEN HE SAW that all his top brass were there, Peppone had the door bolted, and pulled out a small red case from under his desk. Smilzo, Brusco, Bigio, Lungo and the rest of the pulchritudinous gang gazed at the thing with rapt anticipation, and when Peppone lifted the lid, it was Smilzo who exclaimed – 'A portable radiogram!'

'Right!' answered Peppone, plugging the new-fangled radio-gramophone into an electrical socket and playing around with the knobs on the front of the machine.

'But where does the record go?' enquired Bigio.

'What's new is that this radiogram doesn't use records!' explained Peppone. 'It has a steel tape instead, which can be inscribed with music.'[11]

'Whatever will they think of next!' muttered Brusco.

'Well, let's hear it then!' said Lungo.

'Right away,' replied Peppone, who was still twiddling with the knobs.

There was a rustle and then out of the compact unit came Bigio's voice, and then Peppone's and so on. In short, everything they'd just said.

---

[11] Magnetic recordable tape, made of a thin coating of magnetisable metal (steel) on a long, narrow strip of plastic film was developed in Germany in 1928.

'Isn't it extraordinary?' asked Peppone in triumph.

It was a recording machine, pure and simple, but in the Lower Plain that kind of electrical wizardry was as yet unknown. Peppone explained that once a voice was inscribed on it you could keep it and listen to it whenever you wanted. Or you could wipe it clean and make new recordings. Everyone took turns speaking into the little microphone to hear their own voices, and when they'd all had a go, they asked what use might be made of the little gizmo . . .

'To record the speeches of our enemies so we can document what they've said, and to record our own speeches so we can rehearse and refine them. Or, we could record a broadcast from the radio!'

Peppone switched on the radio, let it play for ten minutes, then quickly rewound the tape by reversing it with the rewind button. A few moments later, the machine repeated exactly what they'd been listening to on the radio. To perfection – both words and music.

There followed an extended discussion about the set's possibilities, and all at once Smilzo had an idea.

'I've thought of a brilliant joke! We broadcast a regular piece of normal radio and then, when the chirping bird signals the switchover to our regional channel,[12] we turn off the radio and instead put on a piece of news we've recorded through the microphone. We connect up the tape recorder and put our own news through the loud-speaker in the bar instead of the radio news, and no one will notice the difference. When the news comes on, everyone will swallow it because straight after the official news, they'll get this other piece of transmission we recorded earlier!'

---

[12] This was an interval signal, indicating the switching of broadcast radio channels from the central/national transmitter to regional broadcasters.

An amused grin spread among the gang, and Peppone exclaimed:

'*Ciro degli Oppi!*'

Nothing else needed to be said. They all knew what he meant.

*

Ciro degli Oppi, also a member of Peppone's gang, was fanatical about the football pools. There was never a Saturday when Ciro didn't fill out a coupon. And that was nothing: some people fire off ten or twenty coupons every week. Ciro was the more fanatical because, every Saturday, as soon as he'd handed in his coupon, he immediately started thinking about what he would do with the money he was going to win. And so, when Sunday afternoon came and the radio at the club gave the results of the matches, which were completely different from the ones Ciro had predicted, Ciro flew into a rage, not like somebody who hadn't won, but like somebody who had won and then had his winnings stolen from him.

Every Sunday afternoon, at the social club in the People's Palace, there was the spectacle of Ciro foaming at the mouth like a whole pack of rabid leopards. A few minutes before the radio started broadcasting the sporting news, Ciro would get up from his table and go to lean on the bar counter with the list of football games ready in his left hand and a pencil in his right. The trick they were going to play on Ciro was simply to switch the broadcast with their own, in which the results would match those on Ciro's coupon.

Lungo was the barman at the club and, besides pouring wine and soft drinks, he managed the pools office, so there was no difficulty finding out what Ciro had forecast every Saturday evening.

They studied the operation in the minutest detail, recorded the normal transmission of songs and adverts; and then, on Saturday evening, once they had Ciro's exact list of forecasts, they inserted their news, added another bit of live broadcast, connected the speaker in the bar to the tape recorder and tested the effect (with the sound turned down low).

'Extraordinary!' exclaimed Peppone. 'If I didn't know, it would have fooled me!'

And so, Sunday afternoon arrived: Ciro appeared at his usual time, sat at his usual table and ordered his usual bottle of wine. The loudspeaker broadcast the usual music from the radio and carried on until, at the right moment, Peppone, who was playing cards at the next table, started yelling like a madman at the stupid plays being made by his partner, Bigio, who yelled back even more loudly. Meanwhile, in the other room, Smilzo was taking advantage of the racket to disconnect the radio and attach the loudspeaker cable to the tape recorder.

Nobody noticed because the radio was playing quietly and the racket in the bar was diabolical.

As calm was restored, and the minutes slowly passed, Ciro became ever more nervous. And then *the* moment came and he got up, went over to the counter and took out his list and pencil. Everything had been worked out to the nearest second and, at that precise moment, the voice on the radio announced:

'Sports news . . .'

Everyone in the bar shut their traps and, in the utter silence, the speaker started to rattle off the results of the matches. Ciro feverishly took them down, as he always had done, and when he had finished transcribing the results, he compared them with the forecasts on his coupon . . . And wide-eyed, he began to pant.

'Ah . . . Ah . . . Ah . . .' He couldn't speak and everybody turned towards him looking worried.

'Ciro, what's the matter?'

Ciro waved the coupon in his trembling hand: and three or four men who had also been noting the results checked his entries.

'Would you believe it! This time he's *really* won!' they shouted.

Ciro grabbed a bottle of cognac from the counter, took an enormous swig from it and yelled:

'No more under the thumb! The hard times are over!'

He bolted from the club, cackling manically as he disappeared.

'I was worried he'd have a seizure just winning,' observed Peppone. 'What'll happen when he finds out it was a joke!'

'A joke?' someone said. 'But it was on the radio!'

Peppone went to get the tape recorder and explained what had been going on. Naturally, the interest in that extraordinary machine which recorded voices on a steel tape made everyone forget poor Ciro, because they all wanted to talk into the microphone and play back their own voices.

But all of a sudden a little boy came panting into the bar, sounding the alarm: 'Ciro's gone mad!' he cried.

Ciro lived in a remote little cottage outside town, and Peppone, followed by the whole gang, set off at a run to see what had happened.

They found Ciro still yelling, 'The hard times are over!' And now dancing wildly around a fire that was blazing in the middle of his little yard. His terrified wife was watching him from a first-floor window. When she saw Peppone and his companions, she ran down and explained in an agitated voice, 'He came home, shouting like a madman what he's still shouting – that there'll be no more hard times, that at last his ship has come in. He went upstairs and threw everything out: bed, chairs, tables, sideboard. Then he emptied a can of petrol onto the pile and set it on fire!'

The poor woman seized Peppone's arm: 'Look, look!'

Ciro had grabbed two mattresses and was about to throw them onto the flames, but Peppone and the others were onto him in a moment and ripped the mattresses out of his hands.

'Ciro, have you gone mad?' asked Peppone, taking him by the arm.

'Mad? Mad, because I'm burning this filth?' yelled Ciro. 'Now I've got my millions! Maybe it's only a few, maybe it's a lot, but I've got them! No more hard times . . . I won!'

He wanted to finish the job, and burn everything. It was a mess, a big mess . . . Who was going to tell him the truth? After a few words with one of Peppone's men, Ciro's wife stepped up, and approaching her husband, shouted at him: 'Ciro, stop playing the fool! Don't you understand? It was a joke! You haven't won anything.'

Ciro started laughing. 'A joke? I heard it on the radio! I checked the results and so did the others!'

'Calm down, Ciro,' murmured Peppone. 'It really *was* a joke.'

'But the radio . . .'

'It was a trick, a recording on tape. I'll explain it later, you'll see . . .'

Ciro calmed down instantly. He looked Peppone in the eye, and then all the rest of them.

'A joke . . . Just a joke . . .' he whispered, shaking his head.

He stared for a long time at the bonfire in which the remains of his poor furniture were crackling. He wiped away the sweat that bathed his forehead, then looked Peppone in the eye again.

'If it had been the others, the ones who exploit the people, making fun of our misery, well, all right . . . But that it was you . . . *No!*'

He slowly pulled his wallet out of his pocket, took out his Party card and threw it onto the fire. Nobody dared to move.

'Forget I ever existed!' he shouted bitterly, turning his back on Peppone and going back into his house, followed by his wife.

Peppone remained there, silent and motionless, for a few moments, watching the fire. Then he did an about-face and walked slowly back towards the town with the others.

'It was a stupid joke,' he said shortly before they got there. 'But who could have imagined he'd take it like that? . . . Smilzo, you . . .'

Smilzo, who was as ever, poised for a speedy departure, took a quick step backwards and put his backside well out of range.

'It's not my fault, Boss!' he protested. 'I suggested the idea, *you* thought of Ciro.'

Peppone cut him short. 'Let it go! No one knows anything, nobody saw anything, all right? If the Federation finds out about this, they'll spend the next six months telling us we're morons . . . We'll take him off the Party list, and quietly replace him. He may get over it, after all . . .'

But Ciro didn't get over it. And the reason was that he had burned all his furniture because of that stupid joke; and the story of that sad, ridiculous bonfire was going round the whole district.

Ciro didn't get over it. When his brother's second child was born, he was asked to stand godfather to him at his baptism. When Don Camillo saw him appear before the church, he asked Ciro brusquely, 'How on earth can you have the nerve to show your face here?'

'Don't kick up a fuss, Father,' answered Ciro. 'I'm sorted out now. I burned my Party card and I'm thinking for myself.'

Don Camillo shook his head. 'Yes. You've found God to spite the gang you used to belong to, not from any deep conviction. You've stopped being a bandit, not for any reason than that you hate your gang leader. If they hadn't tricked you with that fake win, you'd still be with them.'

Ciro degli Oppi looked about him.

'Father, if I'd wanted to stay with them, I could have done so.'

'Oh yes, after that splendid joke of making you burn all your furniture – you'd have looked ridiculous from here to the North Pole!'

'I *wanted* to burn my furniture as a good excuse for leaving the Party without any fuss or complications. I knew perfectly well it was a joke. The evening before I'd heard it all from the hallway outside the office. Including the fake broadcast.'

Don Camillo muttered, 'That puts it all in a different . . .'

'But there's no need for you to go spreading it around, Father. The important thing is for *him up there* to know it.'

Of course Christ on the high altar did know all about it and was not in the least offended by being referred to as 'him up there'.

There are fine people among the faithful who kiss the altar steps and call on 'Our Lord Jesus Christ', but wouldn't sacrifice so much as a button for the love of Jesus. Ciro degli Oppi called him what he called him, but for the love of Jesus had sacrificed even his bed, and was sleeping on the floor.

The irony was that sleeping on the floor, his dreams were more sweet and peaceful than if he *had* won a billion on the football pools.

Comrade 'Penèlopo'

DON CAMILLO FOUND himself crossing the piazza just as a small group of Reds were setting up a notice in front of the People's Palace, and so he stopped for a moment to see what it was all about. It seemed to be nothing out of the ordinary:

> *Citizens! Be in the piazza*
> *on Sunday at 3.00pm.*
> *Comrade "Penèlopo"*
> *will speak on the subject of*
> "Defending the Constitution!"
> *Nobody who loves freedom*
> *can afford to miss this!*

'You'd do well to be there too, Father,' said a voice behind Don Camillo.

'And why would I, Signor Mayor?' replied Don Camillo, turning around. 'I don't yearn for the sort of freedom you go on about.'

'Indeed,' muttered Peppone. 'More's the pity.'

'I'm even more sorry, Signor Mayor, because anyone who calls himself Penèlopo must be a very interesting character to listen to.'

'Of course, you'd have found it even more interesting if he'd been called De Gasperi.[13] Never mind, I'll let the

---

[13] Alcide De Gasperi founded the Democrazia Cristiana, the Christian Democrats party, and was Prime Minister of Italy from 1945 to 1953.

speaker know that the town's archpriest doesn't like his name.'

'Don't trouble yourself, Signor Mayor. One man can call himself Penèlopo and be a formidable speaker, while another can call himself Giuseppe Bottazzi[14] and be nothing but a scoundrel. A name means nothing in itself. I noted it because I didn't know there were any Penèlopos around here.'

Peppone shook his head. 'He's not from these parts. He's a great orator from the city. Penèlopo is his *nom de guerre.*'

'I see,' muttered Don Camillo. 'And his real name?'

'No idea,' admitted Peppone. 'Nor do I care. The *nom de guerre* is what counts because a *nom de guerre* is not in the baptismal gift of a priest, it is earned by the personal sacrifice of a Resistance fighter.'

Don Camillo flung out his arms. 'But the resistance is over and it would be good if everyone now introduced themselves by their real names and surnames.'

'That's fine, Father. As soon as Penèlopo arrives, we'll ask him for his papers and send them to you at the presbytery.'

'There's no need, Comrade Mayor. It's of no concern to me personally. Take his papers to the Marshall of the *Carabinieri.* They might well be of interest to him. . .'

Having launched his parting shot, Don Camillo went off to pursue affairs of his own and seemed to have no further interest in Penèlopo, as if he had only used him as a pretext for irritating Peppone, but this was far from the case. In fact, as soon as he arrived back at the presbytery, he sent for a few among his most trusted parishioners and said, 'Do some digging on Peppone and the rest of

---

[14] Nicknamed Peppone.

them at the People's Palace, and try to find out who this Penèlopo is.'

That evening, Don Camillo's task force came to the presbytery and reported that 'Nobody knows anything. Everyone knows him by reputation because he's head of the propaganda unit, but they've never had a chance to speak to him. But he must be right on the ball and very well prepared. Peppone's lot are really excited because they're sure nobody will be able to shout him down.'

Don Camillo shrugged. 'I sense this particular contest is an important one and it's only to be expected that the rabble will roll out their heavy artillery.'

'Perhaps we should bring in a big shot from the city to meet the challenge,' commented one of Don Camillo's men anxiously.

Don Camillo reassured them. 'I'll make a trip to the city tomorrow and find out what's going on.'

Don Camillo did indeed spend the next day slogging up and down the city, and came back highly satisfied.

'Don't give it another thought,' he advised his team. 'Comrade Penèlopo isn't the phenomenon that Peppone's lot think. I was worried he was . . . someone else, but he's actually the one I thought he was. I heard him speak not long ago in the city. As a speaker, he's no great shakes. We must thank heaven that they're sending him and not . . . the man I had in mind. The subject is closed; we'll say no more about it.'

Comrade Penèlopo was forgotten, and so Sunday came around and during eleven o'clock Mass, Don Camillo delivered the sermon, as usual.

'*Fratelli*,' Don Camillo addressed his people warmly, 'every day, every moment, we hear from those weighed down by troubles exclaiming, "Oh, this grain of sand on which we live, what a sad, pitiless world it has become!" And it is true that each morning the newspapers report ever more disconcerting events. Hatred, thirst for vengeance, envy, selfishness, brutality, ingratitude, immorality, dishonesty seem now to be the eternal themes of our daily news stories.

'The world does appear to have become a dark, savage forest populated only by bloodthirsty wild beasts. It is as if the only law left is that of the jungle . . . and that Christian charity is dead.

'But, thank God, this is not true. Faith and goodness live on in our hearts. It as if, when 990 out of every thousand facts reported by our newspapers are stories of wickedness, and only ten of goodness, the 990 do not make us despair of the ten, rather the ten make us forget the 990 and give us hope in a future of peace and goodness.

'In this little leaflet, my friends, there is a story with a truly comforting moral. One that reads like fiction, and yet is wholly true. A rough, unpolished story, but with an ending as sweet as can be, one might almost say enchanting.'

Don Camillo took a paper out of his pocket, unfolded it, and started to read:

'It all began in 1922, when things got pretty hot down in La Bassa. The socialist co-operatives were in full swing, and they were the Reds' real strength in those days. As you can imagine, a situation that was seriously provoking the blackshirts. And once the temperature reached boiling point, the fascists from the city started making sorties into the region with the socialist co-ops their target. The campaign stirred the fire within – as it were that pyre in *Il Trovatore* . . .[15] And it brought about the complete destruction of the communist co-operatives.

---

[15] Manrico's cabaletta from *Il Trovatore – l'orrendo foco di quella pira*.

'Now, during one of those sorties which targeted a certain village, wreckers from the city found the wine and food shops guarded by a small number of determined young men. And one of these young men was a hulking Christian lad with arms like the trunks of an oak tree and with fists he waved like handbags weighing two tons each. And this young man took the worst bully among those city vandals and held onto him while the other blackshirts retreated in their truck licking their wounds, reserving the right to send him back to his natural abode by express delivery. When finally he set the bully boy free, the young lad took care to accompany him for six kilometres, kicking him up the backside to make sure he found his way home in double-quick time.

'Come the final, terminal expedition from the city in August 1922, the liquidators of the Reds' co-operatives included, as you might guess, this fellow who'd been on the receiving end of that six-kilometre kicking, and he sought out that gigantic specimen to give him back with interest the gift he had made him of God's goodness.

'He couldn't find him, but he didn't forget him, and a year and a half later he recognised him in the city, where the big country lad had come to do some shopping, and so organised things that at a particular hour the young man found himself in a quiet, secluded alleyway, blocked at either end by a gang of young toughs wielding heavy sticks.

'The young man received enough kicks to ensure he'd travel, not six, but sixty kilometres without stopping. When it looked as if all the medicine had been dispensed, the lad mumbled, "May I go?"

'"You may!" replied the thug. "But make sure you stay out of my way from now on."

'The young man returned to his hometown, and waited a year before visiting the city again. But evidently someone local was in touch with the city thug – by telephone, telegraph, whatever it might be – for as soon as he emerged from the city tram station, the big lad found himself face to face with him again.

'The thug looked him up and down, smiling smugly.

'"That's a nice jacket," he said. "I like it a lot. If you don't mind, I'll take a little sample," and grabbing one of his lapels, he ripped it from top to bottom.

'Seeing his new jacket ruined so savagely, the young man gritted his teeth but didn't make a move. It would have been a mistake to do so, for the tables had turned and he now knew the thug's full name – he was a big wheel: best to let things be . . .

'So, he left with his lapel dangling down, and it was six months before the feeling of humiliation passed. The next time he journeyed to the city, he did all he could to stay out of sight, avoiding all but the least frequented passageways. But it was in one of these very passages that he ran once more into his nemesis.

'"That's a nice jacket," said the man, just as he had the first time, "I like it a lot. If you don't mind, I'll take a little sample," and grabbing one of the jacket's lapels, he ripped it again.

'This time it was like a piece of flesh had been torn from the big lad's chest, but the Almighty helped him to stay calm. If he had resisted, the other fellow would have had him seen to, big time.

'His eyes filled with tears. "Listen," the big lad said, "I've never gone looking for you. You came to my town to beat me up and I defended myself. You've returned the kicking I gave you a hundred times over. Now leave me alone, I'm just an ordinary working man."

'"I'll leave you alone as long as you keep out of my way," answered the other. "Just get it into your head that, even if a thousand years go by, every time I meet you, I'll help myself to another piece of you."

'Some damned good-for-nothing at home must surely have had it in for the young man, must have been keeping a close watch on him, because whether he travelled by tram or bicycle, horse and cart, or motorbike, every time he turned up in the city, he encountered the bully boy and found himself minus one jacket.

'Years passed and the big lad became a huge man, but whenever he went to the city he still could not escape his sad fate. This went on for ages and when the thug, who now did important work for the Party, was transferred to another city, the big fella felt reborn, and lit a candle for the Madonna.

'But fate again insisted that the matter did not end there, and so it happened that in 1940, when the big man was shopping in the city, he came across a procession. At this time there were almost daily demonstrations in support of a Nazi-fascist victory, but our man could think only of his children and the waste of war. He withdrew into an alleyway to let the procession pass and was standing there quiet as a mouse, doing no harm to anyone, when he got a whack on his head that sent his hat flying ten metres into the air, before a harsh voice exclaimed, "Take off your hat when the flags and banners go by!"

'Our man turned around and found himself face to face with his all too familiar adversary.

'"Ah!" exclaimed the thug, "you've got older, but you haven't changed! The same hopeless subversive!"

'Then he grabbed a lapel of his jacket, and ripped it from top to bottom, just as he had done before. . .

'The war went by as we know it did. And when it ended, the big man, who had fought with the Resistance in the mountains, became leader of the communists in his town. And then he became Mayor. And more years passed. The big man had much to enjoy in his life, but what always stuck in his craw was that damned wretch who had so viciously persecuted him . . . And then, one day, he found the pig-headed bully standing once again before him.'

*

Don Camillo stopped reading and said, 'Understand, my brothers, it had been a dreadful affront and anyone else in that man's position, finding his merciless persecutor in front of him, would at the very least have felt a spontaneous urge to give him a smack on the head. But he didn't bat an eye. He *smiled*, my brothers! He smiled and, turning to his loyal comrades in the piazza, said, "Comrades, I have the honour to introduce the speaker sent to us by the Federation, Penèlopo: also known as Comrade Davide Lagnòlo!"

'He said this and, shook his hand with a smile. . . Yes, brethren, let us forget politics for a moment and remember the man and his fine, big-hearted gesture. Are we not proud that in our mayor, Giuseppe Bottazzi, we have the best in the world! And shall we not fail to recommend him to the commissioners of the *Premio della Bontà* award!'[16]

*

---

[16] There is a possible confusion here that Don Camillo is referring to the St Anthony of Padua Goodness Prize, also known as the Premio della Bontà, but which is for schoolchildren. In fact that prize did not exist in 1953 when Guareschi was writing. It is possible he was referring to a prize created by the municipality in Trieste in 1950 in order to reward at Christmas a person who had performed an act of goodness. For sure, Don Camillo's intention was both paradoxical and ironic, giving the priest control and leaving Peppone no alternative but to act out the part designed for him.

Outside the church, the congregation found some young men selling the pamphlet that Don Camillo had referred to during his sermon. And there they found, besides the story entitled 'Fine gesture by Comrade Peppone', a big photograph of Comrade Penèlopo in uniform as Comrade Davide Lagnòlo.

That Sunday there were people even foregoing their lunch in order to get a good place in the piazza. There were people at every window and even on the roofs. Everyone wanted to see 'what would happen at three o'clock'. Would the rally be postponed? Would Comrade Penèlopo be replaced at the last minute?

At three o'clock on the dot, Peppone mounted the speakers' platform and stood in front of the microphone. The piazza fell silent.

Peppone swelled his chest: 'Comrades,' he said, 'I have the honour to introduce the speaker sent by the Federation: Penèlopo, also known as Comrade Davide Lagnòlo!'

He shook Comrade Lagnòlo's hand, smiling, and then applauded, along with all the assembled Reds.

After the speeches were over, the Reds' top brass toasted Comrade Penèlopo at a reception in the People's Palace. Then Peppone took Comrade Penèlopo into his office. 'Comrade,' he said, handing him a copy of the special publication, 'read this, if you will.'

Comrade Penèlopo read the story very carefully and then handed the leaflet back to Peppone.

'Comrade, do you perhaps believe the fantasies of the reactionary Christian Democrat press?'

'No,' answered Peppone. 'But it is a fact that you tore the lapel off my jacket every time you met me. And the clout you gave me in 1940 is also true .'

Comrade Penèlope shook his head. 'No, Comrade. None of it is true. If it were true, it wouldn't have been printed in a leaflet of clerico-fascist reaction. Everything published by the clerico-fascist press is false.'

Penèlope's reasoning certainly seemed logical to Peppone, but it left him puzzled.

'Comrade,' Penèlopo stated severely, 'our past does not belong to us. It belongs to the Party, and only the Party can make use of it.'

'Our jackets, however, belong to us,' replied Peppone firmly. And seizing a lapel of Penèlopo's jacket, he tore it right off, leaving the strip of cloth in his hand. Comrade Penèlopo did not say a word, but put on his overcoat and buttoned it up to the neck.

'Comrade,' enquired Peppone through gritted teeth, 'do you need me to show you the way back to the city?'

'No, Comrade. You showed it to me once before. I have a good memory.'

*

Don Camillo was warming himself by the hearth in his little dining room when he heard someone tapping on the window. He got up and went to open the door. It was Peppone who, without a word, held out a hand and showed Don Camillo the lapel from Comrade Penèlopo's jacket. Don Camillo spread his arms and, turning his eyes to the heavens, exclaimed, 'Comrade Peppone, pray God the communists don't win. Comrade Penèlopo will never forgive you for his past. Yes, he'll have me hanged, but straight afterwards he'll hang you too.'

'It'll be worth it if I get to see *you* hanged!' muttered Peppone, stuffing Comrade Penèlopo's lapel back under his cloak.

The Canalaccio

THE CANALACCIO WAS a plague upon the people, a wound that spread ever wider, one that nobody could begin to heal, because the Canalaccio belonged to Boccia.

Once upon a time, the Canalaccio had served to drive a mill down at Pioppetta: now all it did was ruin the farms it passed through on its long, tortuous journey.

The waters of the Canalaccio, being indifferent to the sad fate of the mill, had continued to flow. Untouched for twenty years by spade or shovel, the bed of the canal had steadily risen almost to the level of the bank, the water working its way into the humus of the surrounding fields. And when rain or thaw raised the level yet higher, the fields were flooded.

This spelt big trouble, because the world being what it is, water flows downhill, which is why the Canalaccio – designed to collect water from all directions and carry it to Pioppetta – had been excavated in the lowest part of the region. The land nearest to Pioppetta became the drainage basin for the Canalaccio. Already fully saturated and unable to digest the water it had swallowed up, the land here was stuck with it.

Surface erosion and soil degradation caused enormous damage to the farms on the edge of the waterway, but every time the farmers appealed to Boccia to dredge the Canalaccio, he had replied:

'The canal is mine and the fields are yours: sort it out for yourselves.'

No one had ever succeeded in shifting Boccia on this: repeatedly, the farmers affected, having the law on their side, took legal action against him, but they had to desist after making the initial steps in the suit because they soon realised that, while they had the law on their side, he had the money on his.

In this district alone, Boccia owned 1,500 plots of land, and what about the thousands of acres he owned elsewhere? And the big houses in the city? And the cash in the bank? And the assets abroad?

Even the biggest landowner in the area and – after Boccia – the toughest nut of all, chose to sell one of his farms alongside the Canalaccio, rather than tangle with him.

*

When the Reds won the mayoral election and it seemed as if everything was sure to change, a delegation of tenants and sharecroppers went to Peppone and put the problem of the Canalaccio before him.

'The land being ruined by the Canalaccio isn't ours, but we work it. So, anyone who damages the land that we cultivate damages the workers. And since what our farms produce serves the whole Nation, he damages our national heritage too. We have to make Boccia dredge the canal!'

Peppone spread his arms. 'All right!' he replied, 'but how am I going to do that? Boccia doesn't live here. He stays safely out of the country. We can't touch him, and we can't occupy the canal.'

'You could get the work done and then make Boccia pay for it. Seize his farms!'

'We shouldn't get ahead of ourselves. First the Party must win the national elections and then we'll be able to sort the whole thing out.'[17]

But the Reds did not win the national elections and the Canalaccio went on being what it was. The Christian Democrats won, and so the delegation went and appealed to Don Camillo. But he too flung out his arms and shook his head: 'What can I do? A month ago, as soon as I knew Boccia was back in the country, I went to see him and begged him to give the town a thousand metres of land for the nursery school. He looked at me as if I'd asked him for one of his legs. "Are you mad, Father? In times like these?" So, I found the money to buy the land from him, and I went to ask if he'd sell me the thousand metres for the nursery school. He replied that he never sold anything, on principle. I got the Bishop to intervene, and some MPs. Nothing . . . I've written to Rome and they've told me that for the time being he can't be compelled to give up the land.'

But the delegation continued to press Don Camillo, so he petitioned the Ministry of Agriculture, requesting that the Government expropriate the Canalaccio and take over its management. Their response was that the Government had too many responsibilities already and was not, for the present, in a position to take on new ones. So then the owners of the land traversed by the Canalaccio intervened and took the matter to the farmers' union.

---

[17] There are two layers of government to be voted for. The Reds have "*conquistato*" (won, gained, acquired) the *Comune* (the District). This gives them the executive, i.e. it makes Peppone Mayor. Later, Peppone expects to win the *elezioni politiche* as well, the election of local representatives to the national legislature.

'And what can we do about it?' asked the committee. 'Launch a legal action against one of our own members?'

'All you need to do is throw Boccia out of the union and then everything's straightforward,' objected one of the landowners. 'Everyone knows what a hard case Boccia is, and whenever our enemies want to say what farmers are like, they use Boccia as their example. They talk about his selfishness, his stinginess, his bullying, his heartlessness. And unfortunately it's gospel truth because there's not a meaner man on earth than Boccia, and if you want to see people living in total squalor, worse than the worst pigsty, you just go and visit Boccia's estates. He has single-handedly managed to discredit an entire class of people. Kicking him out of the union and suing him would do us all a big favour.'

'A favour to our opponents!' objected the union president. 'We'd become a laughing stock. With Boccia's resources and stubbornness, a legal action against him would go on forever and make no end of a racket, because he'd kit himself out with the best legal team in the universe. And just think what a field day the communist papers would have! How can we, of all people, present the hostile press with an ideal opportunity to turn "The farmers of the Po Valley versus Boccia" into a weekly saga? We don't wash our dirty linen in public.'

The Canalaccio went on being what it was, and day by day it did more and more harm to those who lived in the vicinity. And nobody suffered more harm than poor Bonetti.

*

Bonetti owned two hectares of land in the worst possible position. The little farm had originally formed part of a large rectangular plot, bounded to the north by the Strada Nuoava and to the east by Strada Quarta. And originally the Canalaccio had not passed through it. This happened later, when evidently it was re-dug so that having previously crossed the Strada Nuoava, a little before the intersection with Strada Quarta, it henceforth crossed Strada Quarta a little before the intersection with the Strada Nuoava – the Canalaccio cutting into the rectangular plot in such a way as to chamfer off its north-eastern corner.

So came into being the unhappiest farm in the universe, a triangle with two sides formed by the two roads, with the Canalaccio the hypotenuse. As if that wasn't enough, its little corner was in the lowest part of the large plot, so that when the Canalaccio ceased working as it was supposed to, the two hectares began to retain water until completely saturated.

For Bonetti, who had put a horrendous effort into buying this scrap of land, it was a disaster. It was only to be expected that he became angrier than anybody about the Canalaccio. It's one thing to take fifty grams of bread from somebody who has two kilos, quite another to take fifty grams from someone who only has a hundred.

Bonetti tried everything possible but, on the day his last-resort petition to the Pope was denied, he decided to use his initiative. Whenever he had a bit of free time, he would take his horse and cart to the river and dig up rocks and mud, and then unload them along the edge of the Canalaccio. People asked Bonetti what he was up to, and he answered, 'I'm doing what they do in Holland. I'm putting up a dyke to protect myself.'

This made everyone laugh. The project was fundamentally wrong-headed. Building a little dyke counted for nothing when the bottom of the Canalaccio was almost level with the land, so the water would carry on filtering through underneath his makeshift dyke. If he wanted to protect himself, Bonetti would have to line the Canalaccio underground with a barrier of impermeable cement.

'I know,' answered Bonetti. 'But I'm making the dyke along the bank so that the earth will get compressed under its weight. That way it will become less porous and the water won't soak in.'

At that point people stopped laughing and instead shook their heads, saying that poor Bonetti had gone crazy, and leaving him to stew in his own juice. Bonetti, meanwhile, carried on with his earthworks. Once he had moved a huge quantity of stone and earth to the site, he sorted out what he had and his dyke began to take shape. At that point no one could remain silent. In fact, poor Bonetti had started to construct, not a dyke, but a kind of wall along the Canalaccio – and this was worse than crazy.

But Bonetti remained calm and explained: 'I want to crush the earth underneath. If I make the base too broad it won't compact so well. I need to concentrate the greatest weight on the smallest area of earth.'

People shook their heads and left him in peace, convinced that he was a fool.

But perhaps Bonetti was not the idiot they supposed. One quiet night, when he had finished his great wall, he dammed the canal downstream, just above the little bridge under which the Canalaccio crossed Strada Quarta. Then, after months and months of work, he waited quietly.

What happened was what had been bound to happen. The canal filled up and invaded the base of the massive wall. But Bonetti had constructed the wall's base in a special way, putting large stones on his side and, on the canal side, smaller stones held together with an earth-based mortar. The water quickly moistened the earth and the small stones slipped away. While the large stones, those on the his side, being tied with cement mortar, remained impervious to it, until inevitably – at one fine moment – the wall collapsed into the canal, blocking it from one bridge to the next.

Bonetti finished the job by casting straw and branches under the Strada Nuoava bridge; straw and branches which the water pushed against the rocks and earth of the collapsed wall, sealing even the smallest gaps.

The water began to cover the first farm after Strada Nuoava, then the second, and so on. It also flooded some low-lying roads, and since it was now tipping down with rain, the whole thing was well on the way to becoming a catastrophe.

Bonetti's house was besieged by a crowd of enraged people, yelling, 'We told you it was stupid! Have you seen what your obstinacy has achieved, you old fool?'

Bonetti threw out his arms and let it all wash over him, until finally, hearing himself repeatedly called an old fool, he almost lost his cool.

'I'm neither old nor a fool. I'm forty-nine and it's worked out just the way I wanted. Does anyone care a fig about the Canalaccio? No. Fine, then we need to create a scandal, stir up something that *makes* everybody care. Instead of squawking like a bunch of hens, all of you who live along the canal should do what I do: dam it, and then sooner or later, when the water reaches the roads, someone is going to have to get a move on and put the Canalaccio at the top of the agenda!'

If the *carabinieri* hadn't arrived at that moment, the baying crowd of Bonetti's neighbours would have torn the poor man to shreds. Even after they'd taken Bonetti away to jail, his neighbours remained in uproar, and in their intense indignation went screaming *en masse* to the Town Hall. They were now really out of control, and for the first time in his life Peppone turned pale and acted immediately, ordering a general mobilisation of labourers to go and unblock the canal.

*

Even Peppone went to work at the site: 'The canal must be cleared as quickly as possible!' he yelled. 'Don't spare yourselves! Remember you're on double time!'

At length Smilzo was left to supervise the work, but Peppone had barely got back to his office when Smilzo appeared in front of him. 'I couldn't bear to stay a moment longer,' he explained. 'I've never seen such idle people. Not to mention the trucks taking away the rocks and the earth! Forget paying them double time. What they need is a good kicking! You've got to intervene. They're stealing the people's money!'

'What people's money!' yelled Peppone. '"You break it, you pay for it." That scoundrel who caused all this trouble will pay.'

In due course the rocks and earth that Bonetti had put into the Canalaccio were removed. And in due course, Bonetti was released and allowed to go home. Meanwhile, however, his neighbours had organised a joint action against him.

'He has to pay for the damage he's caused, and so he will.'

Bonetti went to the farmers' union to defend himself, and angrily they threw him out, telling him that if he was mad he should be in the lunatic asylum.

'We cannot condone breaking the law!' they shouted at him. 'We cannot champion such arbitrary abuse of the values by which we live.'

Bonetti was ordered to pay for the damage and the costs. He would have to sell his little farm to get the money. And they laughed in his face when he told them the price he wanted for it: 'You have the brass neck to ask all that for a little bit of land that's no better than a swamp?'

Even at a throwaway price, his land was always going to be worth four million lire: someone turned up offering him two.

'At least two and half!' begged Bonetti.

'It's not possible,' they replied. 'The farm won't yield anything in that state. Who'd want to rent it?'

'I would,' answered Bonetti.

'Good. If the plot yields what you say, then you are to give us at least 5,000 kilos yield for every *biolca*[18]. If you don't, that means the farm isn't profitable.'

Bonetti accepted the tenancy agreement in return for the 2,500,000 lire. The purchaser was a city lady and he met her in the presence of a notary.

'Remember, we expect order and punctuality,' explained the lady when Bonetti had signed.

'I am a gentleman,' replied Bonetti . . .

*

Bonetti and his wife worked their fingers to the bone, even though day-by-day the farm was eaten away by the Canalaccio and drenched as it was, the land produced nothing like 5,000 kilos per *biolca*. Soon Bonetti found himself in trouble. Still, after paying the costs of the clearance work, the legal fees, and damages to his neighbours, he did have something left and always paid the rent on time, taking the loss on the nose.

Eventually he was forced to go back to the commissioners to re-negotiate the rent, but they would not countenance a reduction: 'Who knows that farm better than you? You took it on, which means you knew then its

---

[18] Approximately 75 acres.

true yield. And they gave you the money precisely because you accepted the commitment to 5,000 kilos.'

And so the time came when Bonetti was no longer able to pay, and one fine morning a car stopped in his yard, and out stepped Boccia, who said to Bonetti, 'Choose: either settle the arrears, or vacate the premises!'

Bonetti stammered that he had a contract with Signora So-and-So, but Boccia chuckled: 'That's my wife, and I manage my wife's affairs.'

Bonetti couldn't pay, and received an eviction order for breach of contract. So he made his last stand:

'If they put the farm right for me and dredge the canal, I'll pay everything I owe, both past debts and into the future.'

When they told him the eviction order had already been signed, and he *must* move out, Bonetti shook his head.

'And where am I supposed to go? I'm not leaving here. It'll take the *carabinieri* to get me out.'

The *carabinieri* never came. Two months went by and then a team of builders arrived and, without so much as a by your leave, started to take the roof off Bonetti's house.

'We've got our orders,' they sneered. 'We have to start refurbishing the house for the new tenant.'

Bonetti shook his head. 'You're poor people like me. You shouldn't be helping a bully to do down a poor man.'

'We *are* poor like you,' they replied, 'but we have to work to eat. We can't go without food to do you a favour.'

Bonetti straightway started the search for a little farm to rent, not easy, but at last he found one at Gazzola; only five *biolca* of land, but it would do for him. They came to an agreement, but the owner reserved the right to call in a reference and made some enquiries. The upshot was that when he said it was Bonetti he was selling to, the response came: 'Bonetti? He's a hothead, an anarchist. When he didn't pay the rent on a farm, they had to take the roof off his house before they could get him out! Do you really want a character like that in a house of yours?'

When, in addition to the roof, they also took the fixtures, Bonetti had to leave. He sold everything, and together with his wife he went to live in a hovel in town. He found day-labouring work wherever he could, on the roads, in the fields.

One day Peppone met him and said, 'Bonetti, if you didn't know the upper class before, you do now. So why don't you take against them, why do you not join the struggle of the proletariat?'

Bonetti flung out his arms. 'For the same reason the little fish who's in danger of being eaten by a big fish stays in the water instead of going to live where there's no danger of coming across a big fish.'

Peppone shook his head. 'So, not even Boccia can convince you?'

'No, Peppone, I still believe in divine justice. Boccia wasn't able to convince me that God does not exist.'

Peppone started to laugh. 'Just think how that would amuse Boccia, if he knew!'

'He does know, and it does not amuse him. Along with all those like him, his purpose is to make the little people lose their faith in the power of God. The wealth of the little people is the wealth he doesn't have and can never have, but which he'd love to take away from those who possess it, so that he can bring the greatest possible number of people down to the level of his squalid misery.'

Peppone gave an admiring whistle. 'That's pretty deep. Where did you read it?'

'Nowhere . . . Don Camillo explained it to me.'

'Ah,' chuckled Peppone, 'I might have known! *He* explained it to you.'

'Yes, so what? The important thing is that I understand it.'

Boccia's car went by, and Peppone asked, 'Don't you feel anything inside when you see that bloke?'

'I feel pity for his cursed flesh,' replied Bonetti.

'Did the priest teach you that too?'

'No, I arrived at that by myself,' said Bonetti.

Might

THE FAMILY PEW was in the front row, and it could not escape either Bolgotti or his wife, who was standing stiffly by his side, that Cesarina was not among the girls who had made their Communion.

Neither of them batted an eye. Citizens who fancy they have a name and a reputation to protect seek to maintain their self-control at all costs. The couple behaved as they always did. Once Mass was over they left the church arm in arm, went for their usual coffee, their usual aperitif, chatted a while with their usual friends, and then they went quietly home.

Cesarina was there waiting for them, and seeing them arriving home so tranquil, she heaved a sigh of relief. She had got away with it. But the storm was brewing over her head and it broke after lunch, once the maid had collected the plates and been dismissed.

'Didn't you go to confession yesterday evening?' Bolgotti asked his daughter.

'Of course she did,' exclaimed his wife. 'I went with her to the church.'

'So how is it that you didn't receive Communion this morning?' Bolgotti enquired.

Cesarina was now twenty-two, but she had been brought up in the old way and was terrified of her father. She blushed and then turned pale. 'I felt dizzy just as I was about to take Communion,' she stammered. You could tell from a mile away that she was lying.

'I said I want to know why you didn't take Communion this morning!' shouted Bolgotti banging his fist on the table.

The girl looked at her mother, but encountered two hard, hostile eyes.

'I couldn't,' she whispered miserably. 'The priest did not want to give me absolution. But I haven't done anything wrong.'

Bolgotti sprang to his feet and went over to the girl. He was frighteningly big and tall, and towering over her he made Cesarina feel even more small.

'If he didn't give you absolution, you must have done something wrong!' said the man through clenched teeth.

'I haven't done anything,' gasped the girl. 'It's because of the elections . . . He asked me who I was going to vote for and he said that if I vote for the monarchists he cannot absolve me.'

The man sneered. 'That's quite an excuse. A pity I'm not such an idiot as to believe it. Stop this stupidity and tell me what you've been up to.'

Her mother pounced on the girl and grabbed her by the hair: 'Out with it, you worthless creature! Tell us, or I'll scratch your eyes out.'

'I've told you the truth, I swear!' sobbed Cesarina. 'Go and see Don Camillo, try asking him and you'll see it really is the reason.'

'How can you be so shameless!' roared her mother and slapped her daughter in her fury. 'You're just saying that because you know the priest is not allowed to tell us anything.'

Cesarina seemed like a rag in her mother's hands, and eventually the woman let her go. The girl collapsed onto the sofa and continued to insist that it was the truth, that she hadn't received absolution because she'd told Don Camillo that she would vote for the National Monarchist Party.[19]

'I didn't know it was a sin! I didn't know!' she moaned finally.

Bolgotti, in a fury, grabbed the young woman by the arm and pulled her up. 'You didn't know before Don Camillo told you, but once he'd explained it to you, you did. So all you had to say was, "All right, on Sunday I won't vote for that candidate," and you'd have been absolved. Don't you see that your story doesn't add up? Now come on, out with the truth.'

But even though they beat her almost to a pulp, Cesarina wouldn't give in: she was up to her neck in this sordid little tale and went on repeating that there were no other reasons.

Bolgotti and his wife were going mad with rage, and the girl's stubbornness finally brought them to such a point that the man took off his belt and flogged her with until he was quite out of breath.

'I couldn't,' moaned Cesarina, 'I swore . . .'

'Swore what?' yelled Bolgotti.

'I swore to vote for the National Monarchist Party on Sunday.'

'And who did you swear this to?'

'To . . . someone . . .'

'Someone!' Bolgotti's eyes were bulging. He stood there, thunderstruck, for a few moments, and then fury took over again. He seized a poker that was nearby, in the corner of the fireplace, and took it out.

[19] The *Partito Nazionale Monarchico* (the Monarchist National Party) was founded in 1946, its emblem a royal crown within a star on a blue background.

'Who is this someone? Tell me, or I'll kill you.'

Cesarina told him. What she said actually came out more in sobs than words but, even so, she managed to make it known that 'someone' was a certain young man, a fine young man with whom the girl had exchanged a few words.

'She is having an affair and she didn't even tell her mother!' exclaimed Bolgotti's wife in horror.

The girl was beaten within an inch of her life and then buried under an avalanche of horrible insults.

'That's why the priest denied her absolution!' decided Bolgotti. 'She's compromised herself, she's dishonoured the family! It's got nothing to do with elections!'

It was not possible to ill-treat the girl more than she had been. The beating was a matter of the most delicate technical precision: she was saturated with blows and insults, and now they sent her away.

'Go to your room and don't come down until we call you.'

Cesarina didn't see anyone until Friday evening. Her mother came into her room, threw her something to eat, called her something terrible, and slammed out again. Towards midday on Saturday they brought her a bowl of soup and a little piece of bread: it was her mother again, and again her mother called her the same foul name.

The girl sighed. 'I need to say something to Father.'

Bolgotti came up a few minutes later. 'What do you want?' he asked in a threatening tone.

'I won't vote monarchist, I'll vote Christian Democrat,' replied the girl. 'God will forgive me if I break an oath.'

'And then what?' roared Bolgotti.

'If you let me go to confession, I'll take Communion tomorrow.'

Her mother broke in, saying, 'Don't believe her, she's utterly shameless. It's the same old fairy tale. She hasn't done making fools of us yet.'

'If you take me to church to confess, I'll take Communion tomorrow morning, and then you'll see that I've been telling the truth. If the priest absolves me, it means I've done nothing wrong.'

Her mother again said they should take no notice, but her husband shook his head. 'No, I want to find out how far this girl's insolence will go,' he said. 'I'll accompany you now and tomorrow morning.'

He took her to the church, and waited for her at the door. The girl came out a few minutes later.

'Finished already?' asked Bolgotti sarcastically.

'I had hardly anything else to say. Come with me tomorrow to vote, as soon as they open. I'll take Communion at the eight-thirty Mass.'

She was led back to her room.

'That girl's up to something,' decided her suspicious mother after her husband told her how things had gone. 'In any case, she'll sleep with me tonight. I don't trust her.'

The next day, the Bolgottis left the house at eight, went to vote at the local school, and hurried to the eight-thirty Mass. There, among the other young women, Caesarina made her Communion. When Bolgotti saw Don Camillo offering Cesarina the Host as if it was the most normal thing in the world, he and his wife exchanged glances. When Mass was over, everything happened just as it did every Sunday, only more quickly because it was raining. They went home and all three sat in silence by the little fire, which the maid had lit because it was cold, even though it was early June.

Finally Bolgotti said in a low voice, 'Cesarina, if you had voted for the National Monarchist Party instead of the Christian Democrats, you would have been guilty of a deceit and therefore unworthy to receive the consecrated Host. And likewise your mother and I. . . Instead, we have kept our integrity intact because all three of us have given our votes to the party chosen for us by Don Camillo. We can be proud of this. Cesarina, now that everything is as it should be, may we know the name of the young man to whom you had promised to vote for the Block?'

'Yes, Papa. He is called Gigi Lamotti.'

Bolgotti slowly turned his head to meet the eyes of his wife. 'Gigi Lamotti?' he asked in a low voice. 'The young man who died last month in a road accident at Fiumetto?'

'Yes, Papa. We spoke through the cellar window.'

'Very well, Cesarina,' whispered Bolgotti. 'He was a fine boy. May his soul rest in peace.'

The three of them sat silently by the fire until it went out. And at lunch time they ate nothing.

'There are times when one doesn't feel hungry,' observed Bolgotti. 'It's the excitement of the elections. Politics over-excites us.'

When Bolgotti went to the presbytery it was already dark.

'Is there some news?' enquired Don Camillo. 'Anything wrong?'

'No, Father. Everything is as it should be. Everything has turned out all right in the end. All three of us in the family have a clear conscience because we cast our votes as you told us to. I have come to see you at this late hour because I don't mean to cause a scandal. I want the matter to stay between you and me, Father. I would like to tell you a story under the seal of the confessional. A strange thing, which has happened to us in the past few days.'

Bolgotti began his story in a calm voice, and at the end of it he sighed, 'I don't want to hear what you think about this, Father. All I ask is that you give me a hand loading something onto the truck that's waiting outside.'

Don Camillo followed Bolgotti and made no show of surprise at anything he had said. He gave Bolgotti the assistance he required, and then Bolgotti took his leave.

*

Time passed, and after Mass one Sunday Don Camillo remained to speak to Christ above the high altar.

'Jesus,' he said, 'the Bolgottis weren't in church again today. I think it's unlikely that you'll see them here again. I know their type. Fine, grand people, but blockheads: they cannot think for themselves. I'm sorry about their family pew, too. It's been here since 1805, a hundred and fifty years. They came to take it away one evening . . . In fact, Bolgotti came because he had something to tell me . . .

'Jesus, their house is just opposite the church, on the other side of the piazza, and the window of the first-floor hallway looks right on to the church. The family pew is there now, at that very window, and every Sunday the Bolgottis open the window and follow the Mass from there . . . Old Giuseppina, who cleans for them . . . she told me . . . they do this every Sunday . . . Jesus, I know it's not really in order, but I pray that you will consider them as . . . being present.'

Christ said nothing, and Don Camillo went on, 'Jesus, I do understand, but you need to bear in mind that I am a mere corporal in the ranks. Nothing but the very last wheel on the wagon . . .'

Don Camillo shrugged and then looked up again.

'Jesus, make me not the very last wheel on an armoured car.'

Christ said nothing, and Don Camillo went slowly away, his heart filled with sadness.

The Niche

THE DAY DESOLINA delle Pianche left earthly affairs behind, due to old age, everyone wanted to know, 'What poor creature's going to inherit the Crostone?'

The farm known as the Crostone went to a man from the city, and it didn't take the fine fellow long to realise what kind of legacy he'd been landed with. He arrived at the Crostone one sunny morning by car, with his wife, teenage son and little daughter. Old Goffi, the tenant farmer, was barking poplar poles on the threshing-floor, and scowled when the strangers appeared.

'Good morning,' said the townie, coming up to Goffi with his little tribe trailing behind. 'Is this farm the Crostone?'

Goffi looked him up and down.

'Why?' he asked aggressively.

The visitor was puzzled. 'I'm sorry,' he stammered, 'I've obviously come to the wrong place. I thought this was the Crostone.'

'It is!' shouted Goffi, going back to his pole-stripping. 'So what?'

The visitor looked at his wife, then smilingly explained to Goffi, 'I'm Signora Desolina's nephew . . .'

'If Signora Desolina wants to discuss business, she can come here herself!' shouted Goffi, slicing off the top off the pole with a fierce blow from his pruning hook.

'Signora Desolina is dead,' said the townie.

'About time!' sneered Goffi.

The conversation having reached this point, it was difficult to see how the thread might decently be picked up again, but the townie's wife broke in and explained to Goffi, 'Signora Desolina has died and now this farm belongs to my husband.'

Goffi made no answer and went on with his work.

'If it wouldn't inconvenience you too much,' asked the townie, 'could we take a look at the farm?'

Goffi stuck his hook into the chopping block and set off.

'This is the farm,' he said when they reached the start of a long cart track. 'Two squares: one here, one there. The boundary is that hedge that runs all the way round.'

The townies looked at it. 'Nice,' said the lady.

'Nice to look at,' bellowed Goffi, 'not to work.'

They went back to the farm building and passed through an archway.[20]

'These are the living quarters,' said Goffi, opening an iron door.

'You mean the stable,' objected the lady.

'No!' yelled Goffi. 'These are the living quarters. The stable is the other half!'

He opened the door that was half off its hinges and invited them in.

---

[20] Typically this kind of farmhouse comprised a long building with an arched passage running through the middle which divided the structure into two – human quarters on one side, stables on the other. The *porta-morta* (the rickety iron dead-door alluded to) stood at one end of the arched passage and led to the dwelling quarters.

'Forward, forward, fearless ones! We've lived in this pigsty for years. Come on, Signora, come on, so you can make comparisons with your house in the city. You kids, have you ever seen where poor people have to spend their lives struggling to earn a crust of bread?'

The kitchen was full of people: scowling men, graceless women and a wild, misshapen monster of a boy. The house really was hideous, and the man from the city flung out his arms disconsolately:

'I'm truly sorry, but I only inherited this farm a week ago, and I cannot reason why she let things go like this.'

'If reason is to be left to us idiots,' laughed one of the younger men, 'we reason that you, the master, better *do* something about it!'

The townie was a rather shy and reserved gentleman: 'Yes, indeed,' he said, 'I'll send a surveyor to take a look.'

'And what's a surveyor going to see, that you haven't seen already?' shouted old Goffi.

'Yes, but we need a surveyor to establish the extent of the work . . . make an estimate. I have no idea what it might cost.'

The old man looked at his children. 'He's been given 4,000 acres of land at today's prices, and he's fretting about what it might cost to put the farmhouse right!'

'Maybe he's waiting to inherit the money for it!' sniggered one of the women.

'He doesn't need to!' explained the oldest woman. 'We all know he's got three buildings in the city and a villa by the sea.'

'I'll send my surveyor round tomorrow,' the man assured them. 'What needs to be done will be done.'

The entire Goffi clan crowded round the townies as far as the door, their fate in their hands.

As the car left the farmyard, the lady said, 'If you ask me, sell it straight away.'

'I disagree,' answered her husband. 'The farm is a good prospect – the land is excellent.'

'Those people will squeeze you dry. They didn't even offer us a glass of water. They're low-life.'

'If you live in a tip like those poor creatures you aren't going to be very friendly.'

'Do as you wish. I'm not setting foot in that place again, and I don't want the children there either. They had *L'Unità* on the table. It's a den of Communists.'

'The whole world is a den of Communists,' muttered the man from the city.

*

Two days later, the surveyor arrived at the Crostone, accompanied by an assistant, and measured everything that could possibly be measured.

'And so . . .?' asked old Goffi when they had finished.

'The foundations and walls are sound. The rest is all to be restored.'

'We knew that already. It didn't take a surveyor to work it out.'

'There are technical details in everything,' replied the surveyor. 'When somebody dies, everyone knows he's stopped breathing, but you still need a doctor to write the death certificate.'

'The day's coming when there'll be no need of a technical certificate to prove that a bloodsucker of the people has been dealt with.'

One of the Goffis shouted fiercely. 'We'll do it. We pass the cemetery. Even if we don't have a degree in medicine!'

The surveyor shrugged, got back into his car, and cleared off.

'The only real way to improve that place,' he explained to his assistant, 'would be to put a bomb under the house when they're all in bed. The farm would double in value, at the very least.'

But the owner of the Crostone opted instead for the more conventional plan of issuing precise instructions to the surveyor, and a month later the requisite materials and builders turned up at the Crostone.

'The work will be done in two stages,' the foreman explained to the Goffi family gathered around him. 'First we'll do the new building, and when that's done, you'll move out of the old part and we'll start the repairs.'

He showed them the plans and old Goffi muttered, 'You can see how that monkey's money keeps growing. They're all the same, those cretins from the city.'

Work started on the new part and everything seemed to be going smoothly until suddenly politics exploded upon the scene.

The builders had built the walls almost up to the level of the first floor, when the old man hurled an oath at the bricklayer who was working on what would have been the new entrance way, and demanded:

'What are you doing?'

'Forming the niche,' replied the bricklayer.

'What niche?'

'The one marked here on the plan. The niche for the Madonna.'

Hearing the old man squawking, the whole family arrived *en masse*.

'No niches!' ordered old Goffi. 'Put your Madonnas in the church.'

'*I'm* not putting anything anywhere,' muttered the bricklayer. 'I'm just following the plan.'

'Fill in that hole, or there'll be trouble!'

The foreman appeared and said, 'We're following orders. The owner pays me and I have to do what he wants. Don't talk with us about it, talk to the owner.'

As chance would have it, the owner himself arrived at just that moment, got calmly out of his car and, smiling broadly, went to join the group.

'All going well?' he asked.

'No,' replied Goffi grimly. 'All is going badly.'

'Why's that?'

'No niches, no Madonnas. No politics.'

The owner turned pale. 'What's politics got to do with anything?'

'Everything. If I came to the city and put a niche over your door and stuck Mohammed in it, what would you say?'

'Mohammed? But we're Christians . . .'

'The Madonna is the same for us as Mohammed would be for you. No niches. No Madonnas.'

The owner was a shy, reserved man of few words, always softly spoken, always polite:

'I didn't know,' he said regretfully. 'I'm sorry.'

'No harm done. You don't make the niche and everything's as it should be.'

'I had no idea,' the townie went on. 'I thought you were Christians like me.'

'We are what we are. Subject closed.'

'Subject closed,' agreed the townie. Then, turning to the foreman, he said, 'Stop work. Take down everything that's been done. No point digging up the foundations. But load up all the new and restored materials. From now on I'm only paying for demolition and removal.'

The Goffis were stunned.

'What is this, a joke?' asked the old man finally.

'I never joke,' answered the shy townie politely.

'Don't touch a thing!' yelled Goffi. 'The first man who dares to lay his hand on a single brick goes away with his head smashed in!'

The townie turned even paler. Slowly he climbed the scaffolding, picked up a hammer and began demolishing the newly laid wall. When he was tired, he dropped the hammer and came down.

'I'm sorry,' he exclaimed, 'but Our Lady helped me too often when I was parachuting during the war. I can't commit such an act of disrespect to her.'

The townie walked away, got back into his car and left before the Goffis could open their mouths again.

They recovered their power of speech once the car had left.

'We'll have time enough to settle scores with that vandal,' said the old man. 'As for you, you watch what you do.'

The foreman shrugged. 'I'm not looking for trouble. Don't worry, I won't be setting foot in this place again. Sort it out with him yourselves.'

'The same goes for us,' muttered the builders, gathering up their tools.

'See you again soon!' exclaimed old Goffi. 'You'll see, we'll make that bloke get rid of the niche – every brick of it.'

Three days went by with nobody at all showing up. Then a truck arrived, carrying a dozen young men from outside the region. The Goffis all charged into the yard, but at the same moment four *carabinieri* appeared. The men jumped down from the truck and approached the scaffolding. The one in charge gave some orders and the men set to the demolition work.

The Goffis lost their heads and hurled themselves at the young men, who outnumbered the family and were far too determined. In any case, the *carabinieri* intervened immediately.

'It's oppression! Provocation!' yelled old Goffi in desperation. 'The authorities cannot assist hooligans who come to destroy my house!'

'Nobody's going to touch your house,' replied the leader of the men. 'You'll still have what you had before. We're not taking anything away from you. We're taking away the materials there's no use for, since the new house isn't going to be built.'

'That's what you think!' roared one of the Goffis.

'It's not what I think, it's what the boss says. And when the boss says something, it happens.'

Now Peppone emerged out of the blue, after Smilzo had reported suspicious manoeuvres by enemy forces in the vicinity of the Crostone.

'What's going on?' enquired Peppone, jumping down from his motorbike.

'Boss!' yelled one of the Goffis. 'See what these delinquents are doing! And the *carabinieri* are protecting them.'

'The *carabinieri* do not protect delinquents!' came the voice of the Marshal.

Peppone attempted to calm everyone down.

'Marshal, the intention of this young man is not to challenge the defenders of law and order. I beseech you to consider his exasperation at seeing his home being destroyed at the whim of a landlord. This is oppression, an abuse of power which threatens the rights of the entire working masses. A man's home is his castle.'

'We aren't touching the house,' repeated the leader of the men patiently. 'We're recovering materials that can't be used here but which can be used elsewhere. If the tenant has the right not to have a niche, the landlord for his part also has the right not to build a house without a niche.'

'I've lived in this house for thirty years and nobody has ever forced me to have a place of worship over the door,' yelled Goffi.

'You are free to go on living here without the niche,' came the reply. 'Our boss wanted the niche on the new house. But he never built the new house. If he had, there would have been a niche on it.'

The young man signalled to his companions, and they resumed the demolition. But the work did not go on for long.

'Stop!' shouted Goffi. 'I have done my duty. I have denounced in public the landlord's abuse of power. I need this house, so carry on with the work and build the niche. But understand this, I'm not accepting the Madonna, I'm *suffering* it!'

Peppone approved. 'Bravo! Let the house be built, and put a religious emblem over the door. As they pass by, free people will say, "There's the Niche of the Madonna of Oppression!"'

The young men stopped dismantling the house and left. Building work resumed the next day, and when the house was finished, the landlord turned up with a box. Inside was a little ceramic Madonna, which he placed in the niche.

'She's beautiful!' he observed, once he had climbed down the ladder. 'I'll get away for a bit on Sunday. I want the children to see her. They paid for her.'

The Goffi family pretended not to hear; and maybe they didn't, because they were working furiously to organise the furniture in both the new and renovated parts of the farmhouse.

On Sunday morning, the landlord arrived with his wife and children. He stopped his car in the yard, lifted out his tribe, and headed for the house.

'Look, isn't she wonderful?' he asked the children, pointing to the Madonna in the niche. 'Loo . . .' He broke off, but it was too late. Hideously black and monstrous in the white niche, instead of the Madonna in the blue cloak, there was a bottle with a label saying, Lambrusco. A diabolical abomination which so horrified them all that they rushed back to the car and fled in dismay. The Goffis, hidden behind the shutters, nearly split their sides laughing.

'That'll teach you, you damned swine!' yelled the old man.

The Goffis were celebrating the completion of the new house, and they stayed at the table all day long. And when it was nearly midnight, they all went to bed, stuffed to the gills with food and wine, and the old man stayed by himself, staring at the huge array of empty bottles on the long table. Bottles of black glass, hideously black on the white table cloth.

Momentarily he felt his breath fail and standing up he went out into the yard to fill his lungs with fresh air. Outside, he walked determinedly without looking back; then, after a few paces, he just had to turn and look up at the black bottle in the niche above the door.

The moon shone upon the white façade and lit up the niche, but what happened next was not what he'd expected, not what the old man had hoped for. Goffi did see what was in the niche – the hideous black bottle that he'd put there that morning in place of the Madonna. But every nerve in his body froze.

Then he felt his soul invaded by a tremendous anxiety: the fear of having, at all costs, to stay alive. . .

Labour and Capital

AT THE EXTREME edge of town, in the direction of Torricella, stood the factory owned by a family called Furlan. A foreign name but local people, because the heirs of the late, lamented Vinicio Furlan had been born and grown up here, and Don Camillo had baptised them. In fact, Don Camillo had baptised the factory too. It would never have come into being without his direct intervention.

This is another story from long ago, and it began on the day Furlan Senior turned up in the little town, from who knows where, together with his wife and a down-at-heel little truck, laden with the jumble of a typical itinerant tradesman: ribbons, cotton reels, needles, buttons, thimbles, elastic and so on. He made the town the base of his little peddling trade, and people grasped immediately that, besides an extraordinary readiness to work, the foreigner had a brain filled with decidedly brilliant ideas.

In La Bassa, 'decidedly brilliant' ideas usually go by another name, and people who allow them inside their heads qualify as crackpots. Even so, everyone listens to them sympathetically because down here, people like people with the gift of the gab and with enough insanity to detach themselves from what is taken to be the norm, without going so far as to pass into the *ab*normal category.

Furlan quickly acquired a large group of friends, with Don Camillo at the head of them. Furlan confided completely in Don Camillo because he found that he was better understood in the presbytery than anywhere else. But on the day he hit Don Camillo right in the midde of his chest with his famous plan, the archpriest looked at him as if he was a raving lunatic.

'You are joking.'

'I'm serious, Father.'

'Build a button factory here?' yelled Don Camillo. 'That's not a serious proposition. It's a carnival joke.'

Furlan was prepared for such a reception, and carried on regardless. He took out the notebook containing the whole plan and started to explain it all with great clarity. At the end, Don Camillo spread his arms.

'What can I say? You make it all sound very reasonable . . . No one can deny it. But, even so, I'm telling you, the idea of starting up a button factory here will make people laugh fit to bust a gut. Don't go spreading it around, or you'll end up being labelled as one of the town's weirdos. Keep it between ourselves.'

'Very well,' replied Furlan. 'Let it remain between the two of us. And therefore, since I need to find someone to help me put the thing up, that means it must be you who does it with me, Father.'

Don Camillo laughed. 'Me help you? I am as poor as a church mouse.[21]

'I've got a little money. You can help me by selling me that piece of land you have at Malcantone – on credit.'

'That belongs to the parish. It can only be sold in exceptional circumstances, and you'd need to make sure there was no objection from Rome. It's out of the question.'

'You could lease it to me for ten years. I'd be your tenant, and build the factory, then after ten years I'll either have been successful and be able to give you so much money for your land that it'll bring tears to your eyes, and to them in Rome too, or else I won't be successful and there'll be nothing for me to do but go to Argentina and leave my factory as a gift to the Church.'

Don Camillo leased the piece of land to Furlan and, on top of that, found him the money to finish the factory and buy a few machines. Naturally, when it became clear locally that Furlan was serious about making a button factory, there were two schools of thought: the first maintained that Furlan should be put into a straitjacket; the second, that he was a harmless fool.

The fact is, after ten years Furlan was able to buy the piece of land for so much money that it took the Curia's breath away.[22] And the Church sacrificed nothing for it, because all the sacrificing was done by Furlan and his

---

[21] Guareschi's saying is much more interesting than the English one used, but challenged many Italians, let alone English speakers. The Italian phrase he uses means, 'I have money like a travelling hare': 'Io che di soldi ne ho come una lepre in viaggio'. The 'tableau' of the travelling hare has a particular resonance for inhabitants of La Bassa, indeed it appears to be exclusive to the region. Anyone who has seen a hare sitting stock still, ears pricked, on a deserted, dusty, country road in early summer can relate to the symbol of the animal as a traveller naked to the world, vulnerable, penniless, without pockets or bags to hold money. It occurs again in 'The Inner Sanctum' towards the end of this book, when it is given fuller rein in translation.

[22] The Curia is the administrative apparatus of the Holy See in Rome.

wife. The button factory went full steam ahead, earning itself an excellent reputation.

For the rest of his life, Furlan never made a decision without consulting Don Camillo. The one decision he made for himself proved deadly. And that happened when he and his wife decided to get on a train that was fated to crash straight into another one.

Fortunately, Vinicio's sons were old enough to take over the running of the factory, and the factory continued to prosper.

Furlan's heirs, however, never showed their faces in the presbytery to ask Don Camillo's advice; and Don Camillo never took the liberty of advising the younger Furlans on his own initiative. He confined himself to praying that the Eternal Father would illuminate the minds of the heirs, and that was the limit of what he could do.

But after the war, when the factory was overwhelmed by an avalanche of misfortune, he did of necessity once again become involved in the Furlans' affairs. It was no longer possible to pay the workforce, and after a few weeks the workers decided to find jobs elsewhere. Since ninety percent of the workforce were women, and eighty percent of these went to church every Sunday, Don Camillo took the opportunity to recount the proverb of the countryman who had sown wheat and was now waiting for it to ripen. But it did not ripen because it rained constantly, day and night, when wheat needs only sunshine.

The man waited and waited, but the wheat stayed green because the rain did not stop. In the end the countryman got tired of waiting and cut the green wheat, which meant he lost the lot, the seed for next year's crop included.

Don Camillo's message to the women was clear, and he managed to convince them not to desert the factory.

Indeed, both women and men worked without taking a penny in wages until a loan arrived from Rome.

Then the heirs gathered the workers together and made a very simple announcement: there was enough money to pay them all their back pay. But if they were paid it, this would fill one hole, but it would leave a bigger one gaping wide, and the ship would go down all the same. The factory needed a certain level of liquidity to bring the financial situation back to health. Either they sacrificed thirty or forty thousand lire each, or it was all over . . .

The workers complied and sacrificed thirty or forty thousand lire each. Then, of their own free will, they signed a paper stating that they had in fact received the back pay. And the Furlan enterprise tottered on.

Snatched from the jaws of disaster, the factory gradually put itself back together again, and soon started moving step-by-step ahead, which it continued to do until the day the management dropped another bombshell.

They had done their sums again and told the workers, 'We can no longer keep going as we are. Our competitors are wearing us down because our production costs are too high. We've got to spend less, so we have no choice but to lay off the older workers and take on younger girls as casual workers who will be paid at a lower rate. If the older women want to stay, they'll have to accept being re-hired on a casual basis.'

The women in the firing line tried to make the Furlans understand that this was the final straw, especially as new orders were coming in all the time and they'd been having to do overtime. The Furlans replied that the management had worked very carefully through the accounts and, in order not to lose their clientele, everything had to be arranged as they said . . . whatever the cost.

So the women decided to go on strike in protest: 'Either leave things as they are, or we're not going back to work.'

It was then that Don Camillo felt duty bound to intervene, so he went to see the Furlans to explain the history:

'Your father valued my advice very highly.'

'Unfortunately, our father is dead,' they replied.

'Your father, while he was alive, never forgot that this factory would not have survived, had it not been for my help,' Don Camillo went on calmly. 'It would be good if you did not forget it either.'

'Our father knew his business,' answered his heirs. 'And we know our duty, which is to remember all that we owe to our father, which includes life itself. When all's said, our father, not the parish priest, built this factory.'

Don Camillo took that without turning a hair. 'That's fine, but you should at least be aware that this factory would have closed years ago without the help of these women.'

'By serving the interests of the factory, these women also served their own interests, because if the factory had closed they would all have been out of work. We now know we have to lower our costs if we are to remain competitive. Instead of coming to us, Father, it would be more appropriate if you went to those women and explained that they are making the situation worse by not going back to work. Tell them that if they don't go back to work tomorrow, we're going to start hiring younger women.'

'It would be better if I didn't say that,' commented Don Camillo. 'As it would be better if you, at least for the moment, did not hire anyone. We must leave the possibility of an agreement open. Do you see that?'

'Perfectly,' replied the heirs. 'It means that if we need more advice, we'll come and see you at the presbytery. However, you should give no more thought to this; go back to saving souls, while we get on with saving the button industry.'

Don Camillo went home firmly intending not to concern himself any further with the matter, but two days later he had no choice.

*

News came during the morning that there was an almighty row going on at the factory. 'They've hired girls and now all the striking women have besieged the factory.'

Don Camillo ran to the factory and found the women in a state of great agitation. The *carabinieri* were guarding the gates to stop them entering, but the women wanted to get the scabs out, and Don Camillo had to improvise a rally to ease the tensions. He tried to satisfy both parties, but had to conclude his speech by saying:

'Keep within the bounds of civilised behaviour and the law, and you will have not only me but all fair-minded people to help you preserve your inviolable human rights.'

'Well said!' bellowed a voice that Don Camillo would have been happy not to hear at that particular moment. But there was Peppone, accompanied by a full turnout of his top brass.

'Working men and women!' shouted Peppone, 'Our priest's unequivocal words are extraordinarily important because they demonstrate that the present unrest is not political in nature, as the reactionary bourgeois and ecclesiastical allies of the industrial exploiters would have us believe. If I, the undersigned representative of the Workers Party, said that the Furlans are in the wrong, somebody would make the whole thing political; whereas if the reverend parish priest says it, which filthy reactionary will dare to deny this exquisite act of solidarity? We are entirely without prejudice: we are proud to have by our side in this struggle for social justice, the reverend parish priest here present . . .'

Don Camillo was already ploughing into the crowd in his attempt to melt away into it, while Smilzo, at a sign from Peppone, continued the speech without a break, and Peppone set off in pursuit of Don Camillo, catching up with him as he was about to disappear altogether.

'Where are you going, Father?'

'Where my ministry calls me. I've nothing more to do here. I can't stay, now you've turned up.'

'And why not?' sneered Peppone. 'Can't you stand the competition? You want to have a monopoly over the working class?'

'Don't talk nonsense. I'm leaving because I can't work for an unjust cause.'

Peppone was beside himself. 'Two minutes ago you were calling it an honest cause, and now you're saying it's unjust!'

'Exactly, and it *was* a just cause as long as I was involved with it. Now that you're involved, it has become unjust.'

'Amazing! What am I? A magician?'

'You are a communist, comrade. And every cause you support on behalf of your party is unjust. Or if it wasn't before, it becomes so. Dishonest arguments are anathema to honest causes, and your arguments are all dishonest. Treating a sick or suffering person is an honest cause. Treating him by giving him sulphuric acid to drink is dishonest, because instead of curing him you poison him. I cannot help you poison this honest cause. Goodbye, Lucretia Borgia.'

Peppone swelled up with rage. 'Goodbye ...
Semiramis!'[23] he yelled, putting extra scorn in his voice
to give his reference a better chance of standing up to
Lucretia Borgia. '*You* are the poisoners of the people.
We, on the other hand, fight injustice out in the open!'

'Out in the open, but with a mind closed by ideology,'
countered Don Camillo. 'Go ahead, ruin those poor
women. Today they're more in a mood to listen to words
of fury than words of wisdom.'

'It's no good trying to change your cards once they're
in play, Father,' yelled Peppone. 'It's quite obvious
you're angry because you've lost this affair to me.'

Don Camillo turned around, clenching his fists, and
the two men stood there for a few moments, as if ready
to trade punches. They did not, but when they turned
and went their different ways, their souls were as swollen
with enmity as if they had.

*

The sad goings-on at the factory developed as such
episodes do: once Peppone had exhausted all his arguments, reinforcements arrived in the shape of agitators
sent by the Federation, and the damage became irrepa-
rable with the striking women at the factory gates from
dawn to sunset. And so, weeks went by and the hatred
increased on both sides.

This is how things stood when, one night, Don
Camillo was called urgently to Pioppina because an old
man was dying. He went by bicycle, and set off home
again at about two o'clock. Finding himself passing
Malcantone he noticed that something strange was
happening in the factory. He didn't stop, but at a turning
in the road he slipped onto a cart track and went back on

---

[23] Semiramis is a part mythical part historical woman of the 1st century BC, a
foundling who rose to rule over all Asia.

foot. Surreptitiously, hidden by a hedge, he saw what he needed to see, got back on his bike, and set off again at lightning speed.

Peppone didn't want to get out of bed, but had no choice because Don Camillo threatened to charge down his front door.

'What do you want?' he asked furiously when he found himself standing before the priest.

'Get dressed, and bring down a pair of trousers and a jacket and a hat for me.'

'D'you want a mask too?'

Don Camillo pushed him towards the stairs and soon afterwards, Peppone threw him down the trousers, jacket and hat. They left the house and as soon as they were outside, Peppone planted himself in front of the priest.

'Speak! What's this about?'

'I need you for a just cause.'

'Have you changed your mind, Father?'

'No, the cause is just because I'm back on it, and I'm making use of you the way an honest man might use a poisoned dagger, not to stab someone, but to cut the pages of an honest book.' He explained what he'd seen and Peppone was immediately on full alert.

At the junction they heard a noise and stopped.

'I won't talk. I'll stay in the shadows,' explained Don Camillo. 'But you must do exactly as I tell you.'

A truck turned off the main road, moving with no lights, and Don Camillo said, 'That's it! Go to it!'

Peppone leapt onto the running board on the driver's side, shoved his right hand through the window and grabbed the steering wheel, forcing the driver to brake hard to avoid ending up in the ditch.

'What's going on?' asked the driver, while his passenger tried to get out on his side, only to meet Don Camillo's arm reaching into the cabin. And since the arm ended in a hand the size of a shovel, the smaller man sat back down again.

'Turn around,' Peppone ordered the driver. 'Take that stuff back where it came from.'

'I'm not taking anything back,' answered the driver. 'I don't take orders from you.'

They heard a din suggesting that another vehicle, identical to the first but with a trailer, was getting close.

'Block the road!' commanded Don Camillo, 'I'll deal with this one.'

Peppone jumped down and Don Camillo got in. He must have done it a trifle clumsily, because the driver and his passenger flew out of the other door and ended up on their backsides in the ditch. With the truck to himself, Don Camillo put it into gear, but had to take his left foot off the clutch because he needed it to kick the two men who were trying to get back in. After that everything went swimmingly and off he set.

At the Chiavica junction, he drove left instead of right and so, after a half kilometre he found himself in front of the factory gate. The gate was open and a big truck, the third and last, was about to leave. Don Camillo approached it in low gear and politely induced it to reverse.

At that moment, the truck driven by Peppone arrived.

In the factory's main courtyard, there was yet another, smaller vehicle, and on board were the men who had loaded the three bigger ones and their trailers. It was a big team, none of them local, but Don Camillo was unconcerned.

'Unload everything, lads, and put it all back in its place. I can see you've got a crane, and you look strong.'

'We . . .' began the leader of the team frowning, but Don Camillo interrupted him.

'I'd be happy to give you a hand, if both of mine weren't fully occupied managing this contraption here. I don't want to drop it, it would make quite a bang. It wouldn't do to wake up the whole town and bring two or three hundred people who'd just love to grab you by the pants and chuck you into the Po.'

The team said not a word and unloaded the equipment they had just loaded onto the truck. It took three hours and they worked like the damned. Before they left, Don Camillo asked, 'Where were these machines supposed to be going?' They told him that the Furlans wanted to install them in a town near Bergamo, where labour cost less.

'Right: make sure you don't come back, because if you do you won't leave again.'

They assured Don Camillo they understood, and then left.

When everything was restored to perfect calm, Peppone said, 'Tomorrow I'll call the people into the piazza and denounce tonight's operation. Then the fun will start!'

'Tomorrow morning you will not even show up. Just say nothing, so nothing *starts*. Now stay here on guard.'

'But if . . .'

'At night we'll stay on guard, until everything is sorted out.'

Peppone tried to protest, 'I . . .'

'You are under my orders and you do as I say. That's what we agreed.'

'All right, boss,' roared Peppone, spitting at the ground in fury.

The Great Rain

THAT COMRADE CÀMOLA was one of Peppone's most fanatical followers was neither here nor there. The post of crackpot is never vacant in any organisation, and if Càmola wasn't doing the job, somebody else would have covered for him. The trouble was that, besides being a raving Red, Comrade Càmola was also a sharecropper of Don Camillo.

The little farm of San Michelino belonged to the parish. It fell to Don Camillo to lease it out, and Càmola had been the tenant there for twenty years. Well, when Don Camillo first leased the farm to Càmola, he had not been a communist. Anything but. He loved to call himself 'rural' in the fashion of the 1920s, and took part with passionate enthusiasm in the fascist-inspired Battle-for-Grain to increase wheat production. But after the war, like ninety-nine percent of tenant farmers, he had hoisted the red flag and become one of the most disciplined communist militants.

Don Camillo was most put out the day he had his first fight with the new Comrade Càmola.

'Do me the kindness,' he yelled, 'of explaining how, up until yesterday, you argued with me because I disagreed with your uncompromising Blackshirt fanaticism!'

'I say what I like when I like!'

'And what's the logic now behind what you have to say?'

'The logic that the worker must always be in conflict with the employer who exploits the proletariat,' explained Càmola. 'If the employer is white, the worker must be black. If the employer is black, the worker must be white.'

Don Camillo lost his patience. 'So, according to the logic that the employer can't be an idiot, *I'll chuck you off my land!*'

In fact, it ended up that Don Camillo didn't try to evict Càmola: not only because he knew you can't pull a spider out of a hole, but because, as tenant farmers go, Càmola was no worse than the rest.

He preferred instead to limit his visits to the farm. But since the eye of the tenant makes the absent landlord thin as surely as the eye of the landlord fattens the horse,[24] Don Camillo did, in the event, need to show up all too frequently at San Michelino. And he didn't enjoy that one bit.

The arrangement had its ups and downs, but no major upheavals until everything went pear-shaped over the calf.

Càmola turned up at the presbytery and announced to Don Camillo, 'Father, your calf is dead.'

Don Camillo looked at him in amazement. 'You mean, *our* calf!'

---

[24] Guareschi develops the counterpart to the Italian proverb, 'The eye of the master fattens the horse', introduced in *Comrade Don Camillo* (Pilot Productions, 2017) and gives extra weight to its meaning, namely 'Never do by proxy what you can do yourself.'

'No, Father, *your* calf. There are four cows, two of mine and two of yours. There are four calves, two born to my cows and two born to yours. The one that's died was born to one of your cows, so it's your calf.'

Don Camillo laughed. 'This is news to me, Comrade. We have a shared capital. There aren't two separate categories: your livestock and mine. Every part of that capital is half mine and half yours. So, the dead calf is half mine and half yours.'

'No, the dead calf is all yours, because its mother is all yours,' replied Càmola.

Don Camillo couldn't believe Càmola was serious. 'Among other things, we share a cart. If one of its four wheels breaks, who has to pay? Me, you, or both?'

'It depends,' answered Càmola confidently. 'If one of the yellow wheels breaks, you pay, and if it's one of the red ones, I pay.'

'Comrade, the last I heard, our cart was painted green.'

'You've been misinformed, Father. It's painted half yellow, half red.'

Don Camillo leapt up, took his bike out of the passageway, and rushed to the farm. The cart was indeed painted half red, half yellow.

'What kind of clowning is this?' shouted Don Camillo as Càmola was dismounting from his bicycle.

'It's not clowning, Father. It's a clear definition of responsibilities. In fact, while we're on the subject, you need to get your rear wheel repaired. It's got a cracked rim. If you don't see to it in time and I can't use the cart, I'll charge you for loss of earnings.'

Don Camillo hurtled into the stable to see the dead calf.

'Your livestock is on the right,' explained Càmola.

This couldn't be more obvious: the little boards hanging from the wall above the troughs showed that the two cows on the right were named *Priestess* and *Camilla*, while the two on the left were named *Liberty* and *Justice*.

Don Camillo took a long, hard look at Càmola standing in front of him and concluded, 'There are two possibilities: either you've lost your marbles, or you never had any to begin with, but managed to keep the fact hidden from the general public.'

Càmola clenched his fists threateningly. 'I could teach you a thing or two about how to go on in this world!'

'And I could teach you a thing or two about not going on in it any longer!' replied Don Camillo, grabbing him by his ragged lapels.

The idea of being upended in the dung-heap didn't appeal to Càmola, and he started to shout, which brought his wife and two children running. So Don Camillo let him go, and gave him back his lungs so he could, after all, live in this world a little longer.

'Father,' announced Càmola solemnly when he'd got his breath back, 'from this moment, I and my whole family are on strike. We will only tend to our own animals. If you feel like tending to yours, that's up to you. And get rid of your dead calf, because if it rots and infects the stable, you'll pay for any harm done to my animals.'

This was quite a step to take, and Don Camillo suspected that Càmola had lost his mind, so he didn't press the matter. Instead he got on his bike and sailed off into town.

Peppone was working in his garage and Don Camillo didn't bother to go in, but called through the window, 'Please run over to Càmola's place and tell me what's going on. If he's gone mad I'll talk to the doctor, and if he's just being stupid I'll talk to the Marshal of the *Carabinieri*.

'You go, if you've got time to waste,' answered Peppone.

'I've already been. The best I can do is go back again with you.'

Along the way, Don Camillo gave a blow-by-blow account of what had happened, and Peppone listened to him in silence. When they reached the stable, they found Càmola washing *Justice* and *Liberty*, and completely ignoring *Priestess* and *Camilla*.

'Comrade,' said Peppone, 'tell me exactly how things stand.'

Càmola gave a partial account of events, but in the process confirmed the division of capital and responsibilities he had given to Don Camillo.

'He,' said Càmola, 'sits quietly at home in his armchair, with nothing to worry about because he knows I can't do anything to assert my legal rights. He takes advantage of the fact that I don't have the same means of self-defence as other workers. All other workers, when they want to protest against harassment at the hands of their employers, have the power to strike, but not me! I can't fold my arms and say to my landlord, "Treat me fairly or I won't work!"'

'Yes, you can,' replied Peppone, 'what's stopping you?'

'What's stopping me is the fact that the livestock and crops are half mine, and if I don't look after them, they'll die, and that'll be the end of my capital. So we have to divide up the capital and the responsibility. These are my animals and those belong to the landlord. This is the land I farm for myself and that is the land I farm for the landlord. If the landlord doesn't play fair, I go on strike and stop working his land, and stop looking after his animals.'

Peppone shook his head gravely. 'Your reasoning, Comrade, is just and unimpeachable,' he exclaimed, 'but the damned unjust law says you are wrong, even though you're right, and the capitalist is right, even though he's wrong. This skulduggery will be stopped all in good time, but for now you cannot go *partly* on strike. You have to go completely on strike.'

'What about my animals?' asked Càmola anxiously.

'Legally speaking, it isn't a question of your animals on one side and the landlord's on the other. There's a single body of livestock that's shared. So, off you go. Since I, as a model citizen, concerned for the welfare of the commonwealth, happen to be passing, I shall tend to the cows and calves. With your permission, of course.'

'You have my permission,' replied Càmola.

'And Father, will you permit me to look after these animals in order to prevent the death of a public asset? Or have you changed your mind on that score?'

'Go ahead, if it makes you happy,' answered Don Camillo through clenched teeth.

So Càmola left them to it, and while Don Camillo stood in the stable's central passageway watching him, Peppone finished the work Càmola had started. When he had washed, watered and fed *Justice* and *Liberty* and their respective calves, he stood up and wiped himself down.

'Father, that's all I can do. Since you're here, it would be a fine thing if you were to look after the other cows. When all's said and done, the cattle capital is yours as well as the community's.'

Furiously, Don Camillo set to work while Peppone stood watching him. Finally, once the dead calf had also been dealt with, he got back on his bike and went home, followed closely by Peppone. Before disappearing into the presbytery, he turned and asked Peppone:

'In your opinion, who's been cleverer, him or me?'

'Càmola,' answered Peppone. 'However, while it's true he didn't do the work, he didn't have the consolation I got: seeing a priest work. It's a very rare spectacle,

Father, exceptional, and well worth the price of the ticket.'

*

The next day, Càmola informed Don Camillo that the strike was over. Going back to the farm two days later, Don Camillo noted that the cart had been repainted green, and that the cows on the right and left had reacquired their original, generic names. Clearly, even if it had been with Peppone's help, Càmola had got himself back on the rails. Don Camillo refrained from poking the wasp's nest and returned tranquilly to base.

Two months passed, and it was time for the wheat harvest. Càmola performed splendidly.

Still highly suspicious, Don Camillo thought perhaps he was planning something for threshing time.

But the threshing also went completely smoothly. Don Camillo was present, as he was every year, at the weighing of the grain. The communal part to be stored gets put in the large, better-ventilated granary barn. The part to be sold at market is divided into equal quantities and everyone stores it in their own personal granary. In every tenant farmer's house, there is the master's granary barn, and Don Camillo had his at San Michelino.

Everything proceeded extraordinarily well . . . until the last moment.

When Don Camillo's grain had been properly housed in the Master's Granary, Càmola said, 'I'm sorry Father, but this year we can't do what we've always done before.'

'What do you mean?' stammered Don Camillo in alarm.

'This year you mustn't leave your granary door open, but padlocked and sealed. When it's time to shovel the grain, you'll send one of your men to be present, or be there yourself. Then you'll lock it up again.'

Don Camillo replied that there was no need for all this bother, but Càmola shook his head. 'Father, is your grain entitlement part of the communal capital, or does it belong to you personally?'

'It's mine.'

'Well then, I don't want to be answerable for other people's property. I answer for my own, and for whatever is communal. All right?'

Don Camillo sent for a padlock and sealing wax. It was all completely pointless, but not worth the trouble of arguing about. So when it was time to give the grain its first shovelling, Don Camillo sent the sexton with the key and the wax.

'All well?' enquired Don Camillo when the sexton came back.

'All fine. Padlock and seals.'

After witnessing the second shovelling, the sexton came back to the presbytery rather puzzled. 'I may be wrong,' he said to Don Camillo, 'but this year, because of the heavy rain, the grain was threshed while damp, it looks to me that we're in for a nasty surprise about the size of the yield. But the padlock and seals were exactly as they should be.'

The third time – when the grain has to be shovelled to rid it of white dust infestation – the sexton came back even less convinced than he was before.

'Father, the padlock and seal were in place. Nobody's touched the door because I had left a secret mark, and nobody can have got in through the windows or the roof. And yet I'm sure there's been an exceptional decline in the yield of grain. When you weigh it, you'll see whether I'm right or not.'

'There's no need to be so suspicious,' replied Don Camillo. 'Everyone's had a big fall in yield this year.'

'That's true, Father, but go and take a look at the grain yourself some time.'

Two days later, Don Camillo had forgotten all about it, but he had to hurry over to San Michelino because he'd been told that Càmola had fallen off his motorbike and broken a few bones. Don Camillo set off like a rocket and as he went in to Càmola's house, he met the doctor coming out.

'How is he, doctor?'

'Father, when the Almighty performs a miracle, he really shouldn't do it by saving the skin of a good-for-nothing like Càmola. Nothing serious. A month from now he'll be ready to line up in a march with his red handkerchief, his red tie, his red carnation and his red badge.'

Don Camillo went upstairs. Càmola was in the double bed, all bundled up like a package going by the slow train to America.

'Bad luck, Father,' murmured Càmola, 'no Holy Oil. Wasted journey.'

'Good,' replied Don Camillo. 'Better a live idiot than a dead communist.'

'Why are you insulting me, Father?' groaned Càmola.

'Because you're alive by a miracle and you thank God by making fun of his ministers. Besides banning you from being intelligent, does your party also ban you from being polite?'

'Gentlemen are and always have been,' said Càmola.

At that moment, it started to rain.

It started to rain on the big double bed.

A few drops at first, then cats and dogs.

Hanging from two large bolts screwed into the rafters, there was a broad, deep basket filled with honey, quinces, and so forth. It loomed over Càmola's head, and when the rain had filled the basket, one of its two handles broke and down came bucketfuls of grain through a hole in the ceiling. The grain came pouring through the hole and piled up on Càmola's bandaged and plastered chest.

'A tile's come loose!' shouted Càmola. 'Didn't I tell you a thousand times, if you don't repair this shack, sooner or later I'd be buried beneath it?'

'Don't worry,' Don Camillo reassured him. 'The tiles are so light that they may split but won't fall.'

He stayed there with his arms folded, watching Càmola wrapped like a mummy and unable to move a millimetre, as the pile of grain grew more and more vast, and slowly covered the wretched Càmola.

'Father,' gasped Càmola, 'block up the hole, get me out of this!'

'Of course, the decline we've seen this year in the wheat crop has never been seen before,' observed Don Camillo calmly . . . *'In the wheat crop of the parish priest, that is!'*

The pile of grain on the bed was getting ever more enormous, and Càmola kept moaning.

'A little bit of extra covering when you're in bed is no bad thing,' observed Don Camillo. 'After all, the weather is turning chilly now.'

'Father, help me! Any minute now it'll get into my mouth and I'll suffocate!'

'It'll do you good,' laughed Don Camillo. 'And you'll have struck a blow for the unions against the capitalists!'

'Get me out of this, Father!. . .'

'To run my grain down is one thing: but to fix it so that I couldn't spot any holes or depressions in the mound of grain . . . How did you do it? What method did you use?'

'I can't tell you. My father taught it to me. It's a secret . . . *Help!'*

And then the poor wretch couldn't say a word because the grain had covered his mouth. Only his eyes were visible.

'*How* did you even out the grain you've got here?' yelled Don Camillo, bending over him. 'Are you going to tell me?'

Càmola managed to find the strength to move his head to signify 'No'. Don Camillo grabbed the bed and lifted it. The pile of grain slipped away and when Càmola's head and chest emerged, his mouth was full of it. Càmola started to spit, and at that moment his wife came in.

'Jesus and Mary!' she yelled, 'A tile's come loose!'

'No,' Don Camillo shouted back at her. 'What's come loose is the plug of padding *you* stuffed into the hole, which *you* made in the ceiling.'

Then he turned to Càmola.

'So much for the Battle-for-Grain!' he said.

He went back home and started to think about how the devil that rascal had managed to even out the pile of grain from below so perfectly that the sexton had been unable to tell.[25]

This was the problem!

---

[25] Guareschi wrote that he knew the answer to this, but for obvious reasons kept his own counsel.

To the Piazza

WHEN HE GOT to Magotti's place, the boy swerved hard-a-starboard, pulled up with a bloodcurdling squeal of brakes and stopped with his shoulder glued to the wall.

So as not to waste time while he was perched there on his bicycle, he pulled an apple out of his satchel and started to demolish it. But as he was taking his third bite, his friend Camoni screeched to a halt alongside him and gave his usual whistle.

Magotti kept the two boys waiting less than half a minute and shot out through the gate, already astride his bike. Then, as he poised wobbling in the middle of the road to allow Camoni and Dossi to catch up, a window of the house was flung open and his father put his head out shouting:

'If you see any trouble in the city, run to the station and come home on the first train. Got that?'

'Yes, Papa,' replied the boy, pedalling swiftly off. Round the bend, his two friends caught up with him and Camoni asked what was going on.

'News on the radio,' explained Magotti. 'Seems the students are protesting.'

'If they're protesting it means we will too when we get to the city,' commented Dossi, throwing away his apple core.

'We should protest here!' muttered Camoni.

'Here in the village?' asked Magotti in amazement.

'Of course,' replied Camoni. 'Over there the workers and students are protesting even in the smallest towns. And they're dying too. If we're not cowards, we should be doing something too.'

'It's got nothing to do with being scared,' answered Magotti. 'It's because there are only three of us. We'd get laughed at!'

'That's not so,' said Camoni firmly. 'We aren't the only three who think we should protest.'

The boy was not mistaken: there was at least one other person who held exactly the same view as they did, namely Don Camillo, who from the moment he'd heard the morning news on the radio, had been walking up and down the hallway of the presbytery in the grip of such excitement that he could barely draw breath. It reached the point where Don Camillo *knew* that if he did not take action immediately, his thoughts would breach the bounds permitted to a minister of God and, throwing his cloak over his shoulders, he went out of the door and set off determinedly to get things moving.

A little later, all the bigwigs of the Democrazia Cristiana party, who, summoned by the gravity of the situation, were assembled in the parish office in spite of the early hour, saw Don Camillo appear before them, panting and wild-eyed.

'Gentlemen,' he exclaimed, getting straight to the point, 'we can't sit here twiddling our thumbs watching the murder of people who are fighting on behalf of the entire civilised world. We have to do something at all costs!'

Piletti took it upon himself to speak for everyone else in the room: 'We've already done it,' he replied smiling, and handed Don Camillo a large stamped sheet of paper.

Don Camillo looked at the paper in astonishment. 'What's this?'

'Our manifesto of solidarity,' explained Piletti. 'We wrote it during the night, while you were asleep, and this is the final draft. In a couple of hours, you'll see it posted on every street corner.'

Don Camillo clenched his fists. 'A poster?' he roared. 'The communists laugh themselves drunk with our posters! We have to do something ourselves, not hand the job to the printer. We must show our faces. We need all the decent citizens of the town to get together and march on the People's Palace and tell those scoundrels that they are complicit in murder! We must explain to that godless . . .'

'Father,' Piletti interrupted, 'think about it. Is this really the right time to take to the streets?'

Don Camillo moved into third gear and pushed the throttle to the floor, 'Yes, it *is* time we took to the streets!' he yelled in fury. 'If the spread of Soviet control is enough to bring the Hungarians out on the streets, we must at least take to the piazza and let them know what we think of Soviet repression. If the Hungarians have the courage to fight the armoured cars of the godless, we should, at the very least, have the courage to tell the godless all about it!'[26]

---

[26] The Hungarian Uprising of 1956 began as a student demonstration, which attracted thousands as they marched through central Budapest to the Parliament building, calling out on the streets using a van with loudspeakers. It was the first major threat to Soviet control since the USSR's forces drove Nazi Germany from its territory at the end of World War II. They were fired upon by the State Security Police. One student died and was wrapped in a flag and held above the crowd. The revolution brought the Government down.

Piletti shook his head. 'Father,' he declared in annoyance, pointing to the draft manifesto, 'we have said here everything that needs to be said. And you will find here not only the most heartfelt expressions of solidarity for the oppressed, but also the most severe expressions of condemnation for the oppressors. Why do we need to repeat ourselves?'

'Why should I have to repeat that *we must show our faces*, and not just print bits of paper?' yelled Don Camillo.

The other bigwigs, who up until now had simply observed the discussion, intervened and agreed that Don Camillo's reasoning did make sense.

'Peppone and the rest of them,' said Malocci, 'have to see with their own eyes that there's the vast majority of the population behind the words of our manifesto, not just a printer's piece of paper. The best thing to do is to organise a solemn Mass of universal suffrage and intercession for the souls of Hungary's fallen.'

'Good idea,' agreed Polini. 'A Mass is always a good thing because it's full of meaning without being provocative.'

Don Camillo ran out of patience: 'And why would those damned Communists care about a Mass?'

'They'd care because they'd see all the people going to Mass, and because it would enable you to say a few suitable words,' explained Piletti.

This got Don Camillo foaming at the mouth. 'And who am I saying these "few suitable words" to? The Communists aren't going to come to Mass. Whatever needs to be said must be said to their faces.'

By now the bigwigs were sick and tired of talking and being talked at, so Piletti coldly summed up:

'Let's all do our own jobs, Father. You stick to being a priest, and leave the politics to us.'

'Not when there's an election coming up!' answered Don Camillo through gritted teeth.

He had not the slightest intention of considering the matter closed. But just as Don Camillo was on the point of launching his counter-attack, Malocci, who was standing by the window overlooking the piazza, caught sight of something which so alarmed him that it sent the others running to see what was indeed an extraordinary spectacle.

*

The indignation of the people had taken to the streets and was slow-marching with dreadful tread towards the People's Palace.

And the indignation of the people consisted of three sixteen year-old schoolboys walking side by side: Cino Camoni, Gigino Dossi, and Mario Magotti.

After arriving at the local station to catch the train to the city, as they did every morning, the three boys had not left their bicycles at the usual stand. They had not even dismounted. Instead they had turned around and gone back to the village by a different route. Coming to the house where Camoni lived with his widowed mother, the three of them took advantage of her absence to organise the operation, and now there they were in the piazza in full battle array.

Dossi was in the middle with a horizontally striped tricolour, and Magotti on his right with a placard reading, *Long live the heroic Hungarian revolutionaries*. While on his left Camoni carried another placard: *Down with the Soviet oppressors and their Italian accomplices*.

They were three fine-looking lads, smart in appearance, but as they marched all by themselves in the middle of the large, deserted piazza they seemed that much younger and vulnerable. Yet they marched determinedly towards the People's Palace and had already been spotted by the enemy, for some cheerless faces had appeared at the windows of the little Kremlin, and someone had already come out to stand before the door.

The three boys had also been sighted from the other side of the piazza, but nobody had come out from under the shadow of the arcade. Everyone stayed still, as if at the cinema waiting for the film to begin.

'What do those three idiots think they're up to?' exclaimed Piletti in disgust.

'What they need is a good hiding, and I'd gladly be the one to administer it!' muttered Malocci.

'That would teach them to meddle in other people's business!' added Polini.

Some things are the business of all citizens – boys and women included. The bigwigs of Democrazia Cristiana did not understand this, but Don Camillo, who was not a slave to ideology, even though he was a priest, understood it very well. And he jumped when he saw signs of agitation at the People's Palace.

'If they dare touch a hair on those boys' heads I'll smash them to a pulp!' he yelled.

The room contained a massive oak table with four carved legs like pillars. When the Party bigwigs turned round to see what was happening, the table only had three legs. The fourth had been pulled off by Don Camillo and hidden discretely beneath his cloak. He took the stairs four at a time, dreading that he would arrive too late, but he was not too late. The three boys had just stopped as Don Camillo started to cross the piazza.

They stood side by side a few metres from the People's Palace and, waiting in front of the boys, with their shoulders against the wall of the building and their arms crossed, were Smilzo, Brusco, Bigio and twenty of the ugliest mugs in the whole gang of Reds.

The three boys were unimpressed.

'Long live free Hungary!' shouted Dossi, waving his flag.

'Long live the Hungarian revolutionaries!' shouted Magotti raising his placard.

'Down with the Communist murderers!' yelled Camoni, standing solid as a rock. And the boy's voice vibrated with a venom far bigger than he was.

A shiver ran down Don Camillo's spine as he came within a few paces of the boys and stopped, clinging desperately to the leg he'd ripped off the oak table.

The boys went on shouting and the Reds merely gnashed their teeth, but this was not enough for Camoni, who bent down, picked up a stone and hurled it through the balcony window. Then, hearing the shattering of glass, the Reds started, unfolded their arms, clenched their fists and moved slowly towards the three boys. Don Camillo also moved slowly towards the three boys, but at that moment, as if he'd come out of a hole in the ground, Peppone appeared between the gang of men and the boys. At a sign from their leader, the Reds withdrew to the wall of the Palace. There was a moment's silence, then Camoni looked Peppone in the eye and shouted again:

'Down with the Communist murderers!'

Peppone clenched his fists, nodded towards Don Camillo standing right behind the boys, and asked through gritted teeth, 'Who sent you, lad? Him there?'

'My father sent me,' replied the boy without turning around.

'Move along!'

The command broke the deep silence and everybody jumped.

The long arm of the law had arrived. The officer got off his bike, stood in front of the boys and said in an imperious voice, 'This is an unauthorised demonstration. Disperse! Now!'

The demonstrators cleared off without a protest, not least because the fathers of Magotti and Dossi had now arrived, grabbed their respective sons by the arm, and dragged them off.

Camoni meanwhile left under his own steam: his father did not come and get him because the Reds had killed him in 1945, when the boy was only five years old.

The small Red herd went back into their HQ, while the officer of la Forza Pubblica posted himself on protective duty in front of the building.

The only people left in the piazza, standing face to face, were Peppone and Don Camillo.

'When there's trouble,' said Don Camillo, 'bring in an outsider to help you out.'

'I didn't call him,' retorted Peppone scornfully. 'He came off his own bat.'

'Luckily for you!' said Don Camillo, lifting his cloak and giving Peppone a glimpse of the table-leg.

Peppone turned to go, but then changed his mind, did a quick about-face and said to Don Camillo.

'Just for your information, I don't belong to the conformist tendency. I agree with the Hungarian insurgents.'

'Yes, the way a wolf can sympathise with a sheep being torn apart by wolves,' responded Don Camillo, putting the leg from the parish office table back under the shadow of his cloak.

Motorise the Archpriest

THE BOMBSHELL NEWS of the launch of Sputnik[27] struck Don Camillo a nasty blow in the vitals.

Peppone and his followers had a spring in their step once more, and they were so excited that they made no bones about bearding the lion in his den. Every evening the worst scoundrels in the gang could be found in the courtyard in front of the presbytery, and there they remained in curious contemplation of the sky, searching for a glimpse of the Reds' Sputnik orb, like an Omega moon rising overhead, until that night's 'innocent questioner' would turn up to ask at the top of his voice:

'What are you doing?'

'We're looking to see if an American satellite will pass by,' replied somebody in an equally piercing tone. After which they all walked off singing, ' *Non passa più* . . .'[28]

Don Camillo rode the punch with dignified indifference, but you know how it is: we don't only live in our brains; our vitals play their part. And so it happened one

---

[27] On October 4 1957, the Soviet Union secretly launched Sputnik, Earth's first artificial moon. Powered by a car battery, it passed over the stunned American continent once every 101 minutes and propelled the USSR from backward state to superpower and pioneer of the Space Age.

[28] *Non passa più* was a hit sung by Tony Dallara. 'She doesn't pass my way any more, she doesn't pass by because she isn't mine any more . . .'

morning that the archpriest, finding he couldn't open the cellar door, gave it a furious kick that left him limping.

The doctor prescribed a fortnight's rest. Unfortunately, on the twelfth day, when his ankle seemed back to normal, Don Camillo was called urgently to a remote farm where an old man lay dying. He arrived by bicycle, but taking the cart track, he found his front wheel sinking into mud and to avoid falling he had to dismount sharpish and touched down in the worst possible way, on his bad foot. Worse still, he had to drag himself on foot to the house, which was more than a kilometre away. They took him back to the presbytery and by the time he got home his ankle had swollen up like a football.

He couldn't get out of bed for a week, and in those seven days, Don Camillo's faithful parishioners cooked up far worse trouble for him than a mere sprained ankle.

By the time he was on his feet again and knew what was going on, it was too late. Not only had a committee been set up, and not only had the committee started to collect money, but Peppone's Reds had issued a fierce proclamation denouncing the illegality of this whip-round and mediaeval systems used '*to extort money by moral blackmail for the purpose of motorising a political-ly-motivated priest and facilitating his electioneering. All of which indicates that, whereas in the civilised world of Socialism we work for the Progress of Science, in the capi-talist* Democrazia Cristiana *world* . . .' And so on and so forth.

Thus began the dog-whistling of manifestos and coun-ter-manifestos, and at a moment beneficial to all, Don Camillo intervened. He did not give his approval to the initiative and arranged for the donated money to be returned.

Then old Bosoni came to the surface.

Bosoni was seventy years old, but for at least twenty years he had cut himself off from the world, never moving beyond the confines of his farm. In 1932 his only son, then aged eighteen, went wild with enthusiasm when Bosoni came home with a brand-new three-gear Fiat Balilla. He secretly learned to drive it around the farmyard while his father was in the fields with the farm hands, and when the day came that, in his opinion, he'd mastered it, he plucked up courage at dinner to say, 'Papa, I'd like to have a go in the Balilla. I know how to drive it.'

His father, annoyed, said no. 'You'll drive it after you've done your national service,' he ruled. 'And from now on, you don't touch that car again.'

Bosoni was a man of few words, and there was no arguing with him. What's more, the garage stayed double-locked from that day on, and the key disappeared from view. But the boy had not given up on his project, which had become almost an obsession, and so his mother helped him out.

The boy discovered that whenever his father left the house, he gave the key to his wife, and the poor woman lacked the strength of will to resist the relentless daily badgering from her son. In the end, she gave in and allowed him a brief, five-minute spin.

The boy set off in the Balilla and never came back. Two kilometres from the house he wound up in the canal, couldn't get himself out of it, and drowned. His mother lived for five more years in a state of spiritual torment, and was finally laid to rest in a grave near that of her son.

It was from then that Bosoni no longer left his farm and was forgotten by the town.

He surfaced again only when Don Camillo found himself in the aforementioned spot of bother. When Bosoni sent a cart to fetch him, Don Camillo assumed that the old man felt close to death and wanted to put things straight with God. But he found him in good health, upright as a poplar, and with not the slightest intention of leaving this world.

'Father,' said Bosoni, 'the last time you saw me in church was twenty years ago, for my wife's funeral. You'll see me again when they carry me into the church in my coffin. But in spite of that I want to assure you that I mean no disrespect to God or to you. I read in the paper about all the fuss over the car. You did well to close the idea down. I really liked the way you did that and I would like to demonstrate my support.'

Bosoni got up and walked outside, followed by Don Camillo. His farmhouse stood in a large garden, more a wild wood than a garden and bounded by a high wall. The old man moved through the brushwood that covered the flowerbeds and paths, and carried on until he came to the door of a long, low building set against the wall.

'Once upon a time this was the greenhouse,' he explained as he slipped a key into the lock. 'Once upon a time, when this mess was a proper garden, where you now see a wall, was all windows.'

The door creaked open: it was almost completely dark inside, but as the old man gradually opened the door a large and rather alarming sort of catafalque took shape in the middle of the dusty chamber.

The old man went up to it and lifted a corner of a dark tarpaulin, which covered the mysterious and engrossing object: 'This is the Balilla that my son drove into the canal,' he explained, letting the tarpaulin fall again. 'It's been here exactly twenty-five years. I had it fished out, cleaned up and brought here. Since then I haven't been able to look at it. It's from 1932, but brand-new because I've barely run it in. If you'd like it, I'll give it to you.'

'Why do you want to give it to me of all people?' stammered Don Camillo

'It did great harm,' answered Bosoni, 'and I'd like it to do a bit of good. If you want it, you may have it. Send someone with a truck to pick it up. But tell me beforehand, so I can make sure I'm not at home.'

Bosoni closed the door again and locked it with two turns of his key, which he handed to Don Camillo.

'Well, fine,' said Don Camillo, taking the key. 'I'll be here with a truck tomorrow morning at ten.'

*

The next morning at eleven, Gotti's truck stopped in front of Peppone's workshop. Don Camillo had chosen Gotti on purpose to transport the Balilla because he was part of Peppone's gang. It should be the Reds who motorised Don Camillo, since they had done so much to stand in its way..

'Mechanic!' shouted Don Camillo, getting down from the cabin. 'There's something to unload.'

Peppone appeared in front of his workshop. 'The presbytery's on the other side of the piazza,' he muttered. 'You've come to the wrong door.'

'No, I haven't,' replied Don Camillo smiling. 'At the presbytery we only repair souls. Since this is a car, I had to bring it to someone who repairs cars.'

'I don't have time,' said Peppone.

'I'm in no hurry,' exclaimed Don Camillo.

Peppone spread his arms. 'As you wish . . . Put it there, under the awning,' he muttered, returning to his workshop and going back to work.

This had all been pre-arranged too: a team of fifteen volunteers was at hand, ready to spring into action at a nod from Don Camillo, with girders, ropes and pulleys. It took only ten minutes to position the Balilla under the awning and when everything was sorted out, Don Camillo stuck his head again into the workshop.

'Full service, because it hasn't been driven for twenty-five years,' he explained to Peppone. 'Take a special look at the steering, because the former owner's son probably died on account of a problem with that. I'll take the liberty of looking in every now and then to see how the work's going.'

Peppone carried on working busily at his lathe.

'And "every now and then" would mean *what* precisely?' he enquired.

'Once in the morning, once in the afternoon, and once in the evening, every day. No more than that,' said Don Camillo.

'Starting when?'

Don Camillo shrugged. 'Well . . .' he said, today is Saturday, tomorrow isn't a working day. Let's start next Thursday.'

'All right,' answered Peppone with relief.

To avoid having Don Camillo in his hair three times a day, Peppone would have worked non-stop from Saturday to Thursday servicing not just one Balilla, but four Caterpillars as well.

*

The following Thursday morning Don Camillo appeared in the workshop.

'How's our patient?' he enquired.

'Completely cured,' answered Peppone. 'My lad's just checking the tyre pressures. We had to change the tyres: they'd rotted completely, inner tubes included. We had to replace all of the trim, battery, etc. You'll find all the details on the invoice.'

'And the steering?'

'Sorted out. Although . . .'

In came Spartacus, youngest son of the truck-driver, Goffi, who had brought the Balilla to the workshop. Peppone broke off what he was saying.

'All done, Boss,' said the young man. 'You can try the car out.'

'Good,' replied Peppone in some embarrassment. 'I'm busy here. You do the road test.'

'The young man went back outside to the awning, and then the Balilla was heard starting up and moving away. It was obvious that Peppone had been looking for a pretext to get rid of the boy, and Don Camillo picked up the conversation where it had been left off.

'About the steering, Signor Mayor, you were saying, "Although . . ."?'

Peppone rummaged in a drawer of his work bench and came back with two pieces of iron. 'This is the tie-rod for the steering. Bosoni's boy ended up in the canal because the tie had broken.'

'If the tie was broken,' exclaimed Don Camillo, 'no wonder the boy went off the road.'

Peppone put the broken piece under Don Camillo's nose, and Don Camillo was shocked by what he thought he saw. He put on his glasses. He couldn't believe what he was seeing, and yet it was only too clear.

'The steering failed because somebody sawed this tie half through,' said Peppone. Then he wiped away the sweat that was dripping from his forehead. 'It gave me quite a turn when I saw it,' he added uneasily.

'Old Bosoni has suffered enough,' observed Don Camillo, as if talking to himself. 'He must never know about this.'

Someone appeared in the doorway. It was Gotti. 'Let me have my son for a couple of hours,' he said to Peppone. 'My truck's broken down in Frossi's yard and I need a car.'

'I'll tell him as soon as he gets back,' replied Peppone. 'He's not here now. He's testing the Reverend's car.'

Gotti was thunderstruck. 'Bosoni's Balilla?' he asked clearly distressed. 'But it's dangerous! It's already killed someone!'

'That happened because of a broken steering tie,' explained Peppone. 'The steering's fine now. Don't worry, that was all that was wrong with it.'

Gotti remained speechless for a while, then suddenly gasped, 'We must stop him at all costs! Quick, get a move on!'

He hurtled towards Peppone's motorbike, which was parked outside the workshop door, but Peppone grabbed him and held him back. 'Don't be stupid, Comrade, try to keep calm.'

But, far from keeping calm, Gotti completely flipped.

'I'm not being stupid,' he yelled, trying desperately to break free. 'It wasn't just the steering, I cut through one of the pins . . . on the right . . . front wheel . . . I didn't mean any harm to his son, it was him I was angry with . . . It was him I wanted to bump off, damn him!'

Peppone released him and ran outside. A few seconds later the fully-laden motorbike shot away: Peppone in the saddle, Gotti riding pillion, and Don Camillo in the side-car.

They didn't have to go far. They found Gotti's son at the foot of the slope leading up to the embankment road, fiddling with the engine of the Balilla.

'The carburettor got clogged up straight off,' he explained, 'but I've sorted it out.'

'Well done,' said Peppone. 'But now take the motor-bike and have a look at your father's truck that's stuck in Frossi's yard. We'll take care of the car.'

The young man mounted the motorbike and started it up, but then paused.

'Off you go,' said Peppone.

'Isn't my father coming?' asked the young man.

'No,' replied Peppone, 'he'll join you later.'

Off went the motorbike and the three men were left alone together. Peppone lowered the bonnet and then turned to Gotti. 'You know more about these old machines than we do,' he said in a grim voice. '*You* test it.'

Don Camillo broke in, exclaiming, 'No, I can't allow . . .' but Peppone interjected: 'Leave mechanical matters to the mechanics,' said Peppone firmly. 'You stick to repairing souls.'

Gotti had been standing there, still as a stone, and Peppone hooked an arm around his shoulder and pushed him into the Balilla.

'Get a move on, and push her as hard as you can. Go along the embankment as far as the new Chiavica, then down by the Strada Rotta, round behind the town, and come back on the embankment along the road past the dairy. And keep going till I tell you to stop.

'Go!'

Gotti went, up the hill and along the embankment road.

Don Camillo was still trying to speak, but the expression on Peppone's face was unlike any he had ever seen. And besides, he had a huge spanner in his fist.

'Keep quiet!' he instructed Don Camillo. 'Right now, all it would take would be a word out of place and I'd kill not just one but a whole seminary of priests!'

He walked off, and Don Camillo followed him to the embankment. They waited at the side of the road, and a quarter of an hour later, they heard the Balilla coming along the road past the dairy.

'Faster, damn you!' yelled Peppone as Gotti came past, 'faster!'

The Balilla disappeared and Don Camillo's heart filled with anxiety. He looked up to heaven and joined his hands.

'Stop praying!' yelled Peppone, brandishing his spanner.

'Jesus,' implored Don Camillo aloud, 'don't let the pin break. Do not let this poor man become a murderer . . .'

The Balilla reappeared at top speed and went roaring by.

Then it went past again without Peppone lifting a finger to stop it. He only did so on the fourth pass. Gotti slowed down, and reversed into the road leading down from the embankment, and slowly followed Peppone and Don Camillo who were walking down the slope. When he got out of the Balilla, Gotti looked like a ghost.

'It worked all right for you,' commented Peppone through clenched teeth.

'It worked badly for me,' answered Gotti. 'It would have been better if the pin had broken . . .'

Then he walked slowly towards the town.

Peppone slipped into the Balilla, and sat at the wheel, waving to Don Camillo to get in too.

'It's only a few steps,' replied Don Camillo, 'I'd rather walk.'

Peppone looked at him in disgust and put the car into gear. But before he could even put it into second, the front right wheel came away and continued down the road by itself.

The two men went back to town on foot, saying as little as possible until they reached the piazza.

'As soon as I get home I'm going straight to bed,' said Don Camillo. 'I feel a fever coming on.'

'Me too,' muttered Peppone. 'I'm worried it might be the Asian variety.'

The Little Curate

'Father,' said the doctor sternly, 'if you don't allow yourself to relax, how can my medicine help you?'

'I have been stuck in this bed for twenty-nine days,' replied Don Camillo, 'more cut off from the world than a leper, with no idea what is happening.'

'And what is there to tell you, when everything is going well? If they'd sent a decrepit old man to cover for you, I'd understand your anxiety. But Don Cesare is young, smart and makes himself busy. He knows what he's doing, so why do you go on fretting like this?'

'That's precisely why!' Don Camillo would have liked to answer, because he was eaten up with suspicion that the little curate was too young, too smart and too busy.

But there was something else that made every day of forced inactivity more burdensome to Don Camillo: in all this time, not one of his trusted friends, not even Filotti, had come to visit him. Apart from the curate, the very sight of whom was an irritant; the sexton's mother, who brought him little bowls of broth and mash and milk, and who was deaf as a post and almost completely senile; and the doctor, whose only conversation was about absolute rest, drops and powders, not even a dog had crossed the threshold of Don Camillo's room.

It was as if an impenetrable iron curtain had been created around Don Camillo; this was exactly how it felt, and however hard he tried, he could not work out why they had condemned him to this isolation.

'You have to try not to think too much and to sleep instead, if you want to get well,' the doctor warned again.

Don Camillo nodded, but as soon as the doctor had gone, he started tormenting himself all over again by trying to answer the agonising question, 'Why are they doing this to me?'

The answer came like a bolt from the blue: clear, precise, and beyond all shadow of a doubt. His illness was extremely serious, probably terminal, and they were keeping him in the strictest isolation to prevent anyone from telling him. The revelation turned his heart to ice and for a few moments he went limp as a rag. Then came the frenzy: at all costs, he had to find out what was going on.

Don Camillo's bedroom was above the kitchen, and when he needed something he would bang on the tiled floor with a walking stick tied with string to the head of his bed. Though the old woman couldn't hear him, she still possessed excellent eyesight, and could see scraps of plaster falling off the ceiling, and after giving a yell of acknowledgement, she would come up to the sick room.

Don Camillo grabbed the walking stick and started pounding the floor, but there was no sign of life from downstairs. Then, in desperation, he got out of bed. He had been living for thirty days on broth, fruit juice and little cups of skimmed milk. He seemed to have two rubber tubes for legs, and a foghorn was going off in his head. Clutching the bed, the chairs and chest of drawers, he managed to reach the window that overlooked his garden. The fine and frosty December air, hitting him unexpectedly, took his breath away, but cleared his mind, and eyes. He saw the old woman trudging along the path the Lorini's farmyard to get the milk, as usual, and it was pointless to waste his breath since there wasn't another living soul in the fields.

Don Camillo was about to close the window, when a heartrending lament from the courtyard made him look out again. It was Ful who was gazing at him with imploring eyes, howling fit to break your heart. They had tied him to the plum tree with a piece of rope, which explained why for all those twenty-nine days not even a dog had crossed the threshold of Don Camillo's bedroom.

'Here, Ful! Here!' ordered Don Camillo.

Ful set off like an arrow. The rope became taut and the dog kept pulling, even though he was in danger of being throttled by his collar.

'Here, Ful! Here!' Don Camillo persisted, through gritted teeth.

In a frenzy, Ful redoubled his efforts; then, seeing that it was futile, he set to chewing the rope furiously. It wouldn't have been able to resist him even if it had been made of iron, and sure enough, before long it broke. The little door that opened into the courtyard was ajar, and a few moments later Ful entered Don Camillo's room like a shot from a rifle.

The dog was beside himself and Don Camillo had to allow him to let off steam before getting down to business. As soon as he'd calmed down, the priest fished a piece of paper and a pencil out of a drawer, and scribbled a message which he then wrapped up inside a hankie.

As I've explained before,[29] when Ful wasn't hunting with Don Camillo, he went hunting with Peppone, so that while remaining fiercely opposed in the ideological field, Don Camillo and Peppone shared Ful's annual licence fee.

---

[29] *Don Camillo and His Flock* (Pilot Productions, 2015).

'Take it to Peppone! Off you go!' ordered Don Camillo, putting the little package between Ful's teeth. The dog looked at him in amazement and gave a little whimper to show that he was ready to go to the ends of the earth, but that he needed something more specific to go on.

When he wanted to call Ful home, Don Camillo used a single long whistle, while Peppone used two short ones. Remembering this, Don Camillo took a deep breath and whistled twice. Ful understood and shot off like an arrow.

*

Peppone found Don Camillo lying decorously in his bed, and waited at the door.

'Well?' he muttered.

Don Camillo gave no answer.

'I see,' said Peppone, stepping into the room. 'As the mouth of the tomb opens, the sinner mends his ways and seeks membership of the Communist Party.'

'This has nothing to do with politics,' Don Camillo replied with an effort. 'I'm appealing to your conscience as a man, and I ask you to tell me in all honesty what nobody else will tell me. What am I ill *with?*'

'Father,' muttered Peppone, 'I am a mechanic, and unfortunately you are not a broken-down motor, so I don't know what to say to you.'

'You have a network of informants that reaches everywhere,' insisted Don Camillo. 'How is it possible that you've heard nothing about the parish priest's illness?'

'Parish priests are of no great interest to us. Their importance is relative, given that when one priest dies they give us another one, and so everything stays the same.'

'I understand,' whispered Don Camillo sadly. 'You're trying to tell me I'm done for.'

'If only!' exclaimed Peppone. 'I was merely trying to tell you what everyone in town already knows. You have 'flu, complicated by nervous exhaustion which you inflicted on yourself by rushing around like a madman – pointlessly – during last month's elections.'

Don Camillo shook his head. 'It's not true. If it was, why would they keep me isolated like this, with nobody to talk to?'

'Probably because your condition is more stable when you're silent than when you speak,' stated Peppone.

Don Camillo was suddenly struck by dizziness and his throat felt dry.

'Something to drink, please!' he gasped, letting his head fall back on the pillow.

A moment later, a hand lifted his head, albeit roughly, and another hand brought a glass to his burning lips. He took a long, greedy swallow and immediately felt a surge of heat running from his head to his toes, and the frozen blood in his veins started to thaw. His nerves relaxed and a pleasant confusion numbed his brain.

'What is it?' he asked in a whisper, as his eyes grew heavy.

'A mature rosé. I brought you some in a hipflask. I'll put it here under the bed, beside the little cabinet . . .'

Don Camillo heard nothing more and plunged into a soft, warm abyss of cotton wool.

*

When he woke up it was already dark. He looked at his alarm clock: after ten. He had slept for twelve hours and it must have been deep because there on the bedside cabinet were the broth and milk for his lunch and dinner.

The house was silent. He pushed his left arm out from the covers and reaching down between the bed and the cabinet, he fished out Peppone's hipflask, hauled it on board and took a long swig.

He found himself standing beside the bed, and his feet supporting him pretty well. His head was no longer spinning either, but there was now a tremendous emptiness in his stomach.

He looked with disgust at the broth and milk, and gritting his teeth he started resolutely to walk. He took his time, and the operation was highly laborious, but he managed to attain his objective without tumbling down the stairs.

In the kitchen, he found bread and cheese on the sideboard, and after thirty days of baby food, he experienced once again the pleasure of chewing. Divine Providence helped him find a bottle of good Lambrusco within reach, and so Don Camillo was triumphantly able to complete the best lunch of his life.

Having placated his stomach, a deep, subtle malaise took control of Don Camillo, and the second glass of Lambrusco served only to make it worse instead of better. So he stood up, threw his cloak over his shoulders, went out of the kitchen and shuffled towards the sacristy door.

*

'*Signore*,' said Don Camillo to Christ on the high altar, 'I humbly beg your forgiveness for thinking you had forsaken me. Lord, maybe what I have done will hasten my end, but even if it costs me a month or even a year, or ten, of my life, I'll die happy because I have been able to acknowledge my mistake.'

'Do not torment yourself, Don Camillo,' replied the crucified Christ. 'I was expecting you, I knew you would come. Get up and go calmly back whence you came, because you know now that I'll be with you.'

Don Camillo rose up. Weariness weighed on his back and made his legs ache, but before leaving the church, he wanted to go into the little chapel containing the crib which, for the first Christmas in many years, he had not set up with his own hands.

The doctor was clearly right, Don Cesare was a capable young man. He had laid out the crib with care and truly admirable taste. Don Camillo would never have arranged the lights in such an atmospheric way, and even though the landscape had been made from the usual, time-worn elements, it all looked completely new.

Then suddenly, Don Camillo espied something that made him catch his breath. He thought at first it must be his tired eyes deceiving him, and looked more closely. He had not been mistaken. The two little angels which hovered above the stable roof were the same as every year and were holding the same banner with the same promise of peace to men of good will. But the face and hands of one of them had been painted black.

Black as coal.

'Father!'

Don Camillo started and turned around sharply, to find himself face to face with the curate.

'Why are you here, Father, in this cold? It's madness!'

Don Camillo pointed to the black angel.

'Have you seen this, Don Cesare?' he gasped. 'Who could have done it?'

The curate chuckled. 'I did it, Father,' he explained quietly. 'Christ came to earth for the salvation of all mankind, black people included. Cannot black people enter the Kingdom of Heaven? There is no question of race in the House of God. The Church is with those who suffer and in the world today black people are among those who suffer most. And what about the three Magi who came to adore Jesus? Wasn't one of them black?'

'There is no evidence for that in fact,' answered Don Camillo. 'Saint Matthew simply speaks of "some Magi coming from the East".'

'If, later, the Church felt the need to rule that one of the Magi was black,' replied the curate with some force, 'that surely means it wanted to give a more universal significance to Christianity. Unfortunately, only two angels were available to me. If I had had three, one of them would have been white, one black, and one yellow. It is crazy to ignore China. Seven hundred million souls . . .'

'Souls are pure spirit and not differentiated by colour,' said Don Camillo.

'Then why do you want the angels to be white?' demanded the curate petulantly.

'White is in fact the presence of all colours across the spectrum, it reflects all colours equally,' replied Don Camillo.

The curate grinned. 'Father, we cannot turn a social question into a technical one. The Church cannot sustain itself with sophistries and quibbles. The Church must break out of its mediaeval lethargy and adapt to present reality. The Church cannot go on walking in the clouds, but along the road where men of good will walk. By which I mean not the exploiters, but the workers . . .'

The little priest was quite worked up now, leaping about and gesticulating as he spoke, so it was only a matter of time before he lost his balance and ended up on the floor, but two providential hands emerged from the shadows to catch him and get him back on his feet.

'Take my advice, Don Cesare,' said a fatherly voice, 'and go to bed.'

The little priest tottered off and eventually managed to slip away behind the altar.

*

'What are you doing here, at this hour?' asked Don Camillo.

'I came with the curate,' explained Peppone, coming out of the shadows. 'You know how it is. He's young, not used to drinking, and a couple of glasses left him three sheets to the wind.'

'You mean you picked him up in a tavern somewhere!' exclaimed Don Camillo.

'No, Father. He's a very good young man, even if he *is* a priest. He came to have a discussion with us in the mayoral office. He's had an excellent cultural and political education and possesses a fine sense of democracy and solidarity with the working class. It was a very interesting discussion, with positive outcomes.'

'I see,' muttered Don Camillo. 'You managed to get him drunk.'

'A hangover is not a positive outcome,' said Peppone firmly. 'This, however, *is* a positive outcome.'

Don Camillo moved closer to the lamp so that he could read the sheet of paper which Peppone had passed to him, and found it was an application to join the Communist Party signed by Don Cesare. Don Camillo held the paper over a candle flame and set it alight.

'Go ahead, Father,' said Peppone. 'Even if he'd been sober when he signed it, I'd have burned it myself. Priests are less dangerous as enemies than as allies.'

Don Camillo took the little black-painted angel off the roof of the crib.

'Comrade,' he asked Peppone, 'do you think it'll clean up if I put it in bleach?'

'I dare say, Father,' replied Peppone. 'It's your soul that will always be black, even if you boil it in caustic soda. You need to think about that.'

'No need,' exclaimed Don Camillo. 'I'm cured.'

Before returning to bed, Don Camillo gave the little angel an energetic scrub with bleach, and made it white again. Rather too white, for he had to repaint the eyes, mouth, hair, etc.

But that night Don Camillo slept peacefully, and in the morning he was ready for his first Mass.

A Work of Art

PEPPONE COULDN'T BELIEVE it, and for the first time in his life he was not content to read the news in *L'Unità* and checked what he had read in the other papers. Then, when he was sure that it *was* correct, he felt like going out into the street and screaming. But since he couldn't do that, he drank a bottle of wine instead and went to bed.

He didn't get much sleep, because after a couple of hours Smilzo arrived with the special edition of the *Gazette* and the results from the various districts of the province. It was only Peppone's exceptional constitution that stopped him having a stroke. His district had performed unbelievably well, increasing the Communist vote by more than 25 percent, while the Christian Democrats were down 20 percent. Without a moment's hesitation, Peppone leaped out of bed and ran to the telephone. He got through to the Secretary of the Federation straightaway:

'Comrade,' roared Peppone, 'some bloke wrote a letter to me saying that my kind of propaganda is out of date and counter-productive. *Kindly tell him he's a cretin!*'

The Secretary stammered something, and Peppone barged on: 'Don't bother if it's too much trouble. I'll come and tell him myself tomorrow.'

'No need,' replied the Secretary. 'I'll tell him right away.'

Peppone felt as if someone had taken twenty heavy years off him. And while we can understand his emotional state, we need to bear in mind that the bloke who had written that famous letter to Peppone was one and the same Federation Secretary, and we should perhaps gloss over the fact that Peppone hadn't actually called him a "bloke" but something rather more . . . incisive.

Nevertheless, Peppone was not completely satisfied: something important was still missing, and he ordered Smilzo to 'Nip out and see if Don Camillo is in the presbytery.'

'No point, boss. He's 58 kilometres away.'

In the excitement of the moment, Peppone had forgotten that Don Camillo was 'on retreat' in a remote, squalid little mountain village. But even if they had sent Don Camillo to the top of Mont Blanc, Peppone would still have insisted on flushing him out. *Peppone had won!* But what did his triumph matter without the perceived humiliation of his number one adversary!

'Take a pack of official paper and knock on doors. Get the team to help you. Three hours from now I want to have two thousand signatures.'

'What do I say it's about?' enquired Smilzo.

'Tell them it's for speeding up the provision of a new sports field.'

Smilzo and the team worked their socks off and within the time specified Peppone had a pile of papers bristling with signatures. He called together his most senior comrades and set off with them to the city.

*

It was the third occasion that Don Camillo had trodden the bitter road of exile, and it was the second that

Peppone had knocked on the door of the Curia to intercede on his behalf. But at least fifteen years had passed since the first time, and what's more, there was a brand new Bishop now.

The delegation was admitted without delay, and Peppone got straight to the point:

'Your Excellency,' he said, 'harkening to the lofty word of the Father of Christianity, we are here as peacemakers to ask pardon for our old parish priest who, despite his reactionary mentality, has baptised our children and helped the working people in the difficult times of war and foreign occupation. Forgetting our political faith and remembering only our Christian faith, in the intense atmosphere of coexistence, we ask Your Excellency, in the name of our fellow citizens, for clemency on behalf of Don Camillo.'

Peppone was not Khrushchev's son-in-law, but sometimes it's not the quality of the product that counts, but the colour of the label.[30]

The Bishop would gladly have kept the sheets of paper filled with signatures, but Peppone explained that the townspeople's desire was for these papers to be delivered to Don Camillo, to remind him of his duties as a priest and to restrain him in those moments when his political passion got the better of him. The Bishop praised the wise thinking of Don Camillo's flock, and granted him his pardon:

'Tell your fellow-citizens that they shall have their priest back. I am sure he's learned his lesson. In any case, I shall keep Don Guido on hand to help him and help control him.'

---

[30] In March 1963 Khrushchev's son-in-law and daughter had a 20-minute private audience with Pope John XXIII. It was the first meeting between a pope and a leading figure in the Soviet Union.

Don Guido was the curate sent to stand in for Don Camillo. He was another of those young priests on the left who, by constant yelling and agitation, had made their voices so strongly heard in the chapter that, rather than obeying their superiors, they commanded them.

Most of them were the sons of cowherds and tenant farmers, and during their miserable youth they had built up a tremendous hatred of the land-owning exploiters, which they had chewed over and digested during their long years in the Seminary, and on becoming priests had hurled themselves violently to the left, as if their mission was to exterminate the vile Signori and all their tribe.

These bullet-headed, progressive young priests with their crew-cuts and their hands clammy and cold like eels, terrorised the old parish priests and embroiled them in their cockeyed political project of solidarity with the Reds, thereby taking a mountain of votes from the Democrazia Cristiana party and gaining in return a mountain of votes for the Communists.

These left-wing priests were nothing new. In 1848, the people of Parma had seen them 'armed and enrolled in the National Guard on sentry duty, often banqueting late into the night. They wore black tunics and carried guns and daggers, and to outdo their fellows they would tie a belt around one of their thighs into which they slipped pistols, the way bandits do. They had NCOs and they marched, affecting a military air; they drilled in their barracks instead of tending to the faithful and carrying out their duties in the temple . . .' And what is more, they banded determinedly against the wise old Bishop and attacked him in the 'patriotic' newspapers.

In tempore diluviorum, in every troubled chapter of our history, fanatical young left-wing priests have surfaced: liberationist priests frenziedly waving crucifixes, rifles and daggers.

Don Guido had arrived in Don Camillo's parish with revolutionary ideas, and the first thing he did, purposely choosing a moment when the piazza was at its most crowded, was to equip himself with a ladder and tear down and destroy *coram populo* the huge sign which Don Camillo had attached above the church door, proclaiming the papal decree excommunicating Communism.[31]

*

The little village where Don Camillo had ended up was a place out of time, cut off from the world. No electricity, no drinking water, and no drains. The old stone bridge over the stream had collapsed in 1903 and since then it had been impossible to reach the village by car or cart.

The entire able-bodied population, men and women, was working elsewhere and the village looked as if it had been devastated by cholera, because the remaining resident population consisted of about fifty doddery oldsters, and a similar number of children too young to be dragged off to take part in their parents' adventure in foreign lands. The mail arrived every once in a while, but without newspapers, radio or television, life up here was like being on another planet. Currently, the sole entertainment for the old people was going to church and listening to Don Camillo preach.

Don Camillo had arrived in the village on a Saturday afternoon and, as he was going across the tiny churchyard, a rotten apple (fired from God knows what launch pad) had splattered onto his head. He was already blackened with mud in any case, having slogged for two hours up a mule track carrying a suitcase weighing half a ton. The apple was the last straw. He stood his ground in the

---

[31] The Decree Against Communism was a 1949 document approved by Pope Pius XII, which declared Catholics who professed Communist doctrine to be excommunicated as apostates from the Christian faith.

churchyard, legs apart, and in a voice like a hurricane fired off a tremendous sermon about parental negligence and the ruin towards which the world was careering because children were being so badly brought up.

Not one of the fifty old people stayed indoors. They all came to listen and applauded him wildly.

'At last,' they said, 'we've got someone who calls a spade a spade. And about time too.'

The old people were all in church every morning for six o'clock Mass – as long as Don Camillo preached a sermon.

He lived like this for a month, completely cut off, knowing nothing of what was happening in the outside world. And when he returned to base, he had a surprise that took his breath away.

To tell the truth, Peppone had put on a splendid show. Enormous streamers and posters the size of double-bed sheets spelled out every detail of the Communists' victory and the defeat of the Christian Democrats, and for those with poor eyesight he had organised a highly efficient loudspeaker system.

When Don Camillo had managed to retreat into the presbytery the veins on his neck had swollen up like tree trunks. Finding Don Guido in front of him, he dismissed him forthwith:

'Thank you, my son. You may go as soon as you are ready.'

'I am not going,' replied the young curate. 'The Bishop has arranged for me to stay and . . . help you.'

'I don't need help.'

'The Bishop has arranged for me to stay to help you.'

The discussion ended there because Peppone came into the presbytery with all his top brass.

'We are very glad you're back, Father,' said Peppone. 'Having done our duty by making a substantial offering to the church, we would like you to hold a Mass tomorrow to give thanks to God for the victory he has helped us achieve.'

'It wasn't God who helped you,' declared Don Camillo. 'God never helps those with evil intent.'

'Our intentions are not evil. Everything has been done with respect for law and order.'

'I bet. If you want to thank God, do it privately, on your own account. I can't get Him mixed up in your political antics.'

The curate piped up: 'Excuse me, Don Camillo: this is a victory of the working people over the capitalist exploiters. It is a victory of good over evil. Political labels do not come into it. This being the case, one can and should give thanks to God. If you don't want to celebrate Mass, I shall do it.'

*

The curate could not celebrate Mass the next day because, during the night, the supporting chain of a vault broke, opening up a terrifying crack in the church's roof. It was the sexton who noticed it, but it was the curate, just before 5:30, who brought the news to Don Camillo.

'It had to happen,' commented Don Camillo. 'I've been warning the whole world and his dog about the danger for twenty years. And it's come at just the right moment.'

'So where can we hold Mass?' asked the curate.

'For the time being, at the high altar as usual. You'll have to make do with leaving the congregation outside and keeping the door open.'

'But the crack is right above the high altar!' shouted the curate.

'Don't worry,' Don Camillo reassured him. 'If you don't want to celebrate Mass, I'll do it.'

Don Camillo celebrated six o'clock Mass under the cracked vault. He did it calmly, without haste, stretching it out longer than usual in fact. Afterwards, when the curate told him he'd been taking a pointless risk, Don Camillo calmly explained, 'It was the least I could do to thank God for helping me resist the temptation to answer you in kind yesterday when you offered to celebrate Mass for the Reds' victory.'

'And how would you have answered me otherwise?' sniggered the curate.

With a smack around the head: a slap that echoed now as sharp and clear as a gunshot. An exceptional slap. One in ten thousand, a slap worthy of a Renaissance master. It was a real work of art, and when Don Camillo went to the high altar to explain and apologise, the crucified Christ did not have the heart to scold him for it.

And in any case he was too busy holding up the cracked ceiling, and making sure that no progressivist brick tumbled down onto Don Camillo's head.

Competition

DON CAMILLO HAD not the slightest intention of getting mixed up in a dispute of this kind. It's a fact that disputes between tenant farmer and landlord do not admit intervention from outside, except by trades unions, the *carabinieri* or the ambulance service. But this time, completely by chance, Don Camillo did find himself up to his neck in just such a quarrel and, reluctantly, he had to deal with it.

One summer morning Don Camillo was coming home on his bike along the Stra' Bassa when, as he reached the little bridge by Ca' Vecchia, Bosoni's farm, he saw Bosoni Senior running out of the yard, pursued by his tenant, Spocchi, who was brandishing a three-pronged pitch-fork, plainly burning with the desire to spear it into Bosoni's back.

Don Camillo was caught between the two of them, so he leapt off his bike and hurled it at Spocchi, bringing his homicidal charge to a halt. Don Camillo's intervention not only made Spochi desist from the pursuit of his land-lord, it even revised the tenant's ideas a little.

'That'll do for today,' said Spocchi to Bosoni, 'but make sure you don't show your face here again because the minute you cross that bridge, I'll shove this fork into your belly.'

'Father,' yelled Bosoni, 'you're a witness that I'm being threatened with violence! I'll have him locked up!'

Spocchi slapped his hand against his lower back and sneered, 'I'll stick it right through here. You *and* your witness.'

This annoyed Don Camillo.

'Spocchi, I just prevented you behaving like an idiot and all I get in return is an insult?'

'Yours is the folly, Father, stopping me skewering that pig,' replied Spocchi grimly. 'If you don't want trouble, *mind your own business.*'

'Stopping a man from killing his neighbour is definitely my business, as is clear from the Commandments.'

Spocchi was one of Peppone's hard cases, and like his boss had grown half a foot taller thanks to the millions of votes won by the Communists, but now he made a serious error of judgement. Waving his pitchfork under Don Camillo's nose, he advised the priest *to go to hell.*

Ducking down sharply, Don Camillo managed to grab the fork by its handle, lift its three tines over his head, and rip the tool out of Spocchi's hands. Then he tore the fork off, chucked it away, took a firm grip on the handle, and began to beat Spocchi with it, making it clear that he intended to let the treatment go on for quite some time.

But he had to stop pretty soon because the tenant farmer's wife came running out to protect her husband, allowing Spocchi to cut and run.

Tognina Spocchi was an energetic woman with a quick tongue: 'So are you taking the abusers' side now, Father?'

'Your husband threatened me with a pitchfork, and I defended myself.'

'My husband has nothing against you. He was angry with Bosoni, who provoked him.'

Bosoni jumped up with his eyes popping: 'Provoked him?!' he yelled. '*I* provoked him?! . . . Father, they've bought a Millecento. . .'[32]

'That's getting to you, is it?' sneered Tognina.

'I couldn't care less about the car,' Bosoni went on. 'Buy ten of them as far as I care, but I won't have you putting the car under cover and sticking my tractor in the middle of the yard!'

'Do you expect us to leave a brand new Millecento in the middle of the yard?' answered Tognina. 'The tractor is half ours and half yours. If our half stands out in the open, your half does too.'

'The tractor is all mine!' roared Bosoni, 'because I paid for it with my money, and you haven't given me a single lira for the part that belongs to you.'

The woman laughed gleefully. 'If you want us to work the land, give us the equipment. And thank your God that we haven't cleared off out of here and gone to make our way somewhere else. If you want the tractor to stay under the awning, build us a garage for the car. You're not going to exploit us any more.'

Hearing this talk of exploitation, when Ca' Vecchia barely brought in enough to pay the taxes on it, never mind all the money he'd had to spend on machinery and refurbishing the house and stable, Bosoni cleared off for fear he would end up throttling Tognina.

'Off you go and don't come back till we send for you!' shouted Tognina after him. 'The good times are over for you landowners!'

Don Camillo couldn't help putting a word in: 'Tognina, why don't you stop and think for a moment before you speak? It seems to me that the landowners' happy days ended quite a while ago. You've got the radio,

---

[32] 1958: The Fiat 1100/103 D came with a Millecento script (1100 spelled out in Italian) on its centre, and 'stepped' chrome spears on the sides.

a television, a washing machine, a fridge, a fur-lined coat, that brand-new car: you have nothing to complain about.'

'We had plenty to complain about for too long,' stated Tognina. 'It's only fair that we've finally got a few good things now.'

'Nobody's saying it isn't. I'm only saying you should be happy.'

Tognina put her fists on her hips. 'No, Father!' she squawked. 'That, my dear sir, is where you're wrong. It isn't enough for us to be better off. It's time the others were worse off: the *Signori* pigs. We want to see them in poverty. We need to take everything away from them: farms, house, money, car, jewels, clothes. They have to die hungry.'

'I don't see how other people's misery is any use to you,' muttered Don Camillo.

'It's of moral use!' stated the woman. 'The triumph of justice: it's the great gain that honest working people have won. You yourself teach in church that God rewards the good and punishes the wicked. Therefore, the punishment of the wicked is the good worker's greatest reward.'

The logic of this "therefore" could have been debated for a month. And then there was the definition of have-nots as *good*, *honest*, and the haves as *wicked*: which needed a bit of fine tuning too. But Don Camillo let it go, and decided to save the subject for his sermon next Sunday.

And besides, he didn't want to get in too deep with Tognina. Spocchi was one of Peppone's hardliners, as has been said, but Tognina's solidarity with her husband only went so far, because she kept herself in the Eternal Father's good books and never actually voted for the Reds.

*

A week later, Tognina went to confession with Don Camillo and after carefully listing all her sins, she said she was very happy because now she could at last vote the same way as her husband.

Don Camillo hadn't expected this, and was briefly lost for words: 'Tognina, what are you thinking of? I've explained to you over and over again that if you vote Communist you'll be excommunicated.'

'The excommunication has been withdrawn!' objected the woman.

'Says who?'

'If it hadn't been, how could the Pope receive Khrushchev's son-in-law?'

'The Pope has been to visit the thieves and robbers in Regina Coeli prison. Does that mean he's on their side, and the Commandments about stealing and killing don't matter any more?'

'Even in the papers . . .' began Tognina.

'The laws of the Church aren't made by journalists,' said Don Camillo, dismissing Tognina and telling her that, because of her sin in voting for the Communists, he couldn't give her absolution.

*

Tognina surfaced again a week later. She appeared in front of Don Camillo as he was positioning a new candelabra on the high altar.

'The priest at Torricella had no difficulty absolving me,' she explained. 'He's younger than you, more modern, less partisan. You're getting left behind. You'll lose all your customers if you don't keep up to date.'

When Tognina had gone, Don Camillo knelt before the high altar and, turning his eyes up to the crucified Christ, said, 'Lord, it wouldn't matter if my congregation went to another church instead of coming here. The important thing is that they carry on going to church and stay in touch with God.'

'It is also a good idea for priests to stay in touch with God,' Christ replied.

'. . . Naturally,' agreed Don Camillo.

The Travelling Comrade

THIS STORY COMES to us from the strip of land along the south bank of the Po, all strictly bounded east and west within the Duchy of Parma, Piacenza and Guastalla,[33] and touched on its southern edge by the brand-new Autostrada del Sole[34] which cannot contaminate it, since for most of the year the road is hidden under thick fog.

The story is so freshly minted that two-thirds of it has yet to happen, but these parts *will* happen and so we are presenting it as if it already has happened, from beginning to end.

It begins one day when Don Camillo was visited by Licotti, a sometime small farmer who had sold his plot while the land was still worth the trouble of working it, and had started making knick-knacks out of Bakelite in a woodshed. Now, ten years on, here he was heading up an industrial complex for producing plastic artefacts employing 300 workers and administrative staff – a big

---

[33] This is of course La Bassa, the Lower Plain, where almost all Don Camillo stories are set.
[34] The 754 km motorway, the spinal cord of the country's road network, which connects Milan with Naples via Bologna, Florence, and Rome. Work began on it in 1956, and the entire motorway was opened in 1964.

operation which earned him millions, along with a heap of worries and troubles which cost him his sleep.

Don Camillo was touching up two little wooden angels from the high altar with a tiny brush when Licotti came straight to the point.

'I need your help, Father.'

'To count 10,000-lire notes? Can't you do it on your own any more?' enquired Don Camillo with a mocking laugh. He disliked the man because of his stinginess.

Licotti explained that he was talking about the famous European Nations football match between Italy and the Soviet Union. 'It's an opportunity not to be missed,' he exclaimed. 'I'm sending Tacconi, at whatever cost.'

Don Camillo made a grimace of disgust. 'That waste of space? Send him to hell, not to Moscow! Even the Soviets would find that bonehead too much to cope with.'

'If it comes to that, they'd find him too much to cope with in hell too,' answered Licotti.

He was right, because Comrade Tacconi, a senior shop steward at 'Licotti SA', was as Red as he was stupid, and not even the Devil himself would have such a trouble-maker under his feet.

'So send him,' muttered Don Camillo. 'It's your money. What's it got to with me?'

'I need you to talk to the landowners here. The idea is to collect two or three million lire so we can send a nice little group of communist comrades, including the most fanatical, to have a look in person at the so-called workers' paradise. You see, the point would be – this is what I've told Tacconi – that they can then come back and report publicly on what they've actually seen: it would be a fantastic piece of propaganda.'

'Maybe,' admitted Don Camillo,' but it's no concern of mine. When it comes to telling Reds to go and jump in the lake, I'm always up for it. But abroad? . . . No. My personal geography is very limited.'

Licotti, who liked to speak his mind, said, 'I don't know what goes on inside priests' heads. They claim to be fighting communism, and say they're all for hanging communists, then the next minute they're putting them in the Government.'

'That may be so. But on the other hand, you won't find a single priest who's fighting the communist peril by entrusting the job to travel agents.'

'Sometimes I wonder who could possibly have licensed you to be a priest,' muttered Licotti, retreating in disgust.

'You're not the only one,' whispered Christ on the high altar.

And all Don Camillo could do was bow his head and say nothing because, in his conversation with Licotti, he had followed the emotional promptings of his anger and not his brain.

*

Comrade Tacconi left for Moscow a whole week before the match to give himself time for a good look at the communist paradise. And then came the match, and Don Camillo met Licotti a few minutes after it became known that the Italian bunglers had suffered a heavy defeat.

'What a good idea that was,' chuckled Don Camillo, 'giving a crazy Bolshevik the chance to see his Bolshevik comrades beating Western capitalism.'

Licotti shrugged. 'Yes, but it would have been a brilliant double blow if our lot had won!'

In fact, the adventure, which had cost Licotti many thousands of lire, ended much better than could reasonably have been expected. It turned out that when Tacconi came back, he showed himself to have travelled without blinkers and with his brain switched on.

'Sporting victories matter,' he said when he reported back to Licotti and the public at large, 'but you can't eat them. Bread is in terribly short supply over there, and most of the people are dressed in rags.'

'How can this be?!' exclaimed Licotti with feigned incredulity. 'People who have split the atom, and conquered space, and are soon going to land on the Moon?'

'Sputniks and cosmonauts are important too,' replied Tacconi, 'but you can't eat them either. The reality is quite different. And so is the propaganda. If we went by the propaganda, God knows what marvels we'd have found in Moscow! According to the propaganda and the movies, you might think that in the USA they live off the fat of the land; and then you find that some Americans are dying of hunger and others are hanging negroes from lampposts in New York . . .'

The industrialist guffawed. It was obvious that, for all his know-it-all manner, Tacconi was as naïve as they come, a little fish too eager to take the bait.

Licotti sneered. He wasn't the only person listening to him. Tacconi was holding forth in the Bar Molinetto, which was packed with people.

'Tacconi,' said Licotti, 'your job was simply to tell us what you saw in Russia. You've kept your word. On the same conditions, I'm sending you for a fortnight to the USA. That way you can compare the Soviet paradise with the capitalist hell.'

A lot of people laughed, but Tacconi was nonplussed and said nothing.

'I understand,' chuckled Licotti. 'You're afraid . . .'

'No I'm not,' declared Tacconi. 'I'll do it.'

A month later, Tacconi left for New York. On his return, he didn't even dare to show his face, and when he finally turned up in a packed Bar Molinetto, he turned as pale as a Bolshevik washed in Omo.

'Well?' enquired Licotti ironically.

'It's an extraordinary country,' Tacconi admitted.

Then he recounted all the marvels he had seen and touched with his own hand. He carefully reported the wages, the cost of living, and the condition of the workers.

Licotti let him speak, and then concluded:

'So, which is better, the Soviet paradise or the capitalist hell?'

Tacconi turned red and the veins of his neck bulged. 'It's got nothing to do with hells or heavens,' he yelled. 'The truth is simple: if Khrushchev hadn't betrayed the spirit of the October revolution, the Soviet Union would be better off today than America!'

People started jeering and Tacconi leapt up like an enraged tiger: 'There's nothing to laugh about! Look at what's happened in communist China because Mao hasn't betrayed Lenin and Stalin!'

'Oh yes, of course!' trilled Licotti. 'Mao's China, where the best thing the Chinese can do is drop dead! It's the empire of misery! . . .'

'I wouldn't say that,' exclaimed an authoritative voice. It was Don Camillo, who had happened to be passing. 'Tacconi is right when he says that propaganda is one thing, and truth another.'

Licotti stared at Don Camillo. 'I'm amazed to hear that from you of all people.'

'You wouldn't be amazed if you had been in the city last week like me, and heard a missionary priest who's just come back from Mao's China. A huge amount has been done from the point of view of mechanical progress and material benefit. They've got things that even the Russians and Americans still don't have.'

Tacconi was triumphant.

'It must be tough for you to find that the Father agrees with me!' he said, turning to Licotti.

And Licotti, who was an impulsive character, shot back:

'Here's a challenge for you, Tacconi. I'll send you to China for a fortnight, same conditions.'

'You're on,' said Tacconi darkly.

*

The big difficulty was how to get into Mao's China. But Peppone, as soon as he heard what Tacconi had been saying, solved the problem by throwing him out of the party as a "Chinese heretic" and even announcing the fact in the newspaper. Armed with this certificate of merit, Tacconi easily made it into Albania, and then on to China.

And being such a smooth operator, he managed to come back too, and held his third mass gathering in Bar Molinetto.

'Well?' asked Licotti ironically for the third time.

'What's most incredible,' declared Tacconi, 'is seeing how such a honey-pale people can bear such black misery. . .' And he heaped condemnation on Mao and his China.

Licotti was of course triumphant, and meeting Don Camillo the next day, he said, 'Did you hear what Tacconi said last night?'

'Yes, I heard him.'

'So doesn't that mean your missionary priest is either a liar or soft in the head?'

'No, it means he doesn't exist. I made him up.'

'What for?'

'So you would finish the job by sending Tacconi to China.'

Licotti said he couldn't make head or tail of what Don Camillo was talking about. But Don Camillo cut him short and went to let off steam before Christ at the high altar.

'Lord,' he said, 'Tacconi, a Bolshevik to the marrow, who would happily eat bishops and bourgeois factory owners for breakfast, is sent by his bourgeois capitalist boss on a jolly to Russia and then to America. Later, as he speaks well of Mao, he is expelled from the Soviet Communist Party, and Licotti, his capitalist boss, compensates him for the moral damage this has caused Tacconi by promoting him to Foreman and raising his salary. His expulsion from the Soviet Party then also gets him the pass he needs to travel to China, which again he does at the expense of his capitalist boss. When he returns, he speaks ill of Communist China, and communist Mayor Peppone rewards him by re-admitting him to the Soviet Party and promoting him to deputy trustee of the local Section. Now, Tacconi is thinking about how to persuade Licotti to send him to Cuba for a fortnight . . .!'

'I do not understand why you are telling *me* all this,' said Christ.

'Because I'd really like to go travelling too, but how can I do it, given that in order to find a capitalist to fund me I need to become a communist enemy of capitalism and of God?'

'*I* cannot tell you,' replied Christ smiling. 'Politics are a mystery to me.'[35]

---

[35] Don Camillo does find a way to Soviet Russia, of course, in *Comrade Don Camillo* (Pilot Productions, 2017).

The Inner Sanctum

'CAN I BE of service, Father?'

Don Camillo, who was tidying up the presbytery garden, recognised the voice immediately, and didn't even turn around.

'Not me. But *you* could serve yourself an ounce of shame for posing such a question.'

After what Ciapón had got up to, Don Camillo had 100,000 reasons for thinking it took some brass neck to address his parish priest so congenially.

Up until a few years ago, Ciapón had been the most sober, honest man in the entire universe. He had never annoyed anyone, and nobody understood why, during the 1948 election campaign, Peppone's gang of thugs had ambushed him at dusk, beaten him almost to death, and left him lying in a ditch.

Equally inexplicable had been Ciapón's sudden departure one night, after he was back on his feet again, when he'd loaded all his odds and ends onto a cart and set off to a destination unknown..

Then, as unexpected as it was again inexplicable, he had resurfaced ten or twelve years later. No longer working as a casual farm hand, he went around with a little truck collecting old iron, and made his official reappearance on the day of the *Festa de L'Unità*, turning up in the piazza with a big bandanna around his neck and a bundle of copies of *L'Unità* under his arm.[36]

*

Ciapón was still the guarded fellow everyone had known, and so the reason for his new political affiliation and the mania that went along with it remained a mystery. Coming upon Don Camillo one day, Ciapón at first gave him a wide berth, as if afraid of catching the priest's eye, but maybe because of the light dusting of purple-gold mist that clothed the scene on that sleepy November afternoon, Ciapón threw caution to the wind and spoke to Don Camillo as if 'times past' were but yesterday.

'Father,' Ciapón said, showing him a large cylindrical object, 'in my attic, I found a saint who might be of interest you.'

'As far as saints are concerned, we've got a full house,' replied Don Camillo. 'And in any case, we don't use the communist party as a supplier.'

But Don Camillo's brusque response did not put Ciapón off.

'This has got nothing to do with the communist party. Just one honest scrap merchant,' replied Ciapón sharply. 'As I see it, the parish priest of a town whose patron saint is San Michele should be interested in a picture of San Michele.'

The whole San Michele thing was indeed a thorn in Don Camillo's side, because even though San Michele was patron saint of the parish, the church no longer owned an image of him. *Temporibus illis*, there'd been a big fresco in the church which portrayed San Michele. It had been a good painting, but a leaking roof and an

---

[36] The Festa de *L'Unità* refers to the many local festivals and the annual national festival in a designated city organised by the communists, with *L'Unità*, the focus.

especially hard winter had cracked the plaster on which it was painted and San Michele had fallen to bits. All Don Camillo had left were the wretched fragments, and when he consulted experts to see about restoring the fresco, they had just shaken their heads sadly.

So now, hearing about Ciapón's picture of San Michele, Don Camillo set aside the man's history and made a beeline for the door to the presbytery.

'Let's see it!' he said brusquely.

Once in the dining room, Ciapón removed the wrapping paper of his big package and revealed a large, rolled-up oil painting on canvas, dirty but in excellent condition. All it took was a gentle wipe with a damp cloth to reveal such a convincing San Michele that it brought tears to Don Camillo's eyes.

'How much do you want?' asked Don Camillo begrudgingly.

'Ten Masses for the blessed soul of my brother Antonio.'

The priest's eyes bulged like the headlamps of a Landau convertible.

'But no! Do you not remember your brother?'

'Of course I do,' answered Ciapón. 'Why would I forget him?'

'Because you now march under the Soviet flag, and your brother was taken prisoner fighting against the Russians, and died of hunger and cold and ill-treatment in a Russian concentration camp. Your duty now as a militant communist is surely to forget a brother like this . . .'

Ciapón clenched his fists. 'Father,' he said, 'you don't know the whole story, but I'll tell it to you in confession and you will not repeat it to anyone.'

Ciapón wiped the sweat from his forehead.

'In March 1948, Peppone's gang gave me a beating that almost did for me. You know this, but you don't know why. My brother was reported to be a prisoner somewhere in Russia, but I knew for sure that he'd been murdered in one of Stalin's lagers . . . If you remember, the Liberals had stuck posters pretty well everywhere, with a photo of Stalin and the words, '*A vote for Garibaldi is a vote for Stalin*' . . . Seeing that murderer's ugly mug all over the place tipped me over the edge. I was passing the station forecourt with a shovel over my shoulder and there was a pile of cow dung this big! – steaming fresh, because Tognini's cart had just gone by. It was lying right there, below Stalin's phizog. It was a serious provocation, Father, and I couldn't resist. I scooped up the cow's doings and painted it over that no-good's face. That little witch Gisella[37] saw me and ran straight to the People's Palace. The same evening they came round and gave me a going over, and I decided on a change of air. So you do understand my situation, Father.'

'I understand it up to a point,' replied Don Camillo. 'What I don't understand is how you can have a brother murdered by the Reds, and get your own bones broken by the Reds, and then end up joining the Reds.'

'Father!' shouted Ciapón, 'you don't understand because you are politically . . . you let your feelings *rule* your reason. But I am not: I *use* reason. And my decision is the *result* of reason. I joined the communist party, Father, as soon as news of de-Stalinisation starting to spread. That way, I could come back home without a blot on my character and no fear. I learned Khrushchev's anti-Stalin speeches off by heart – the cult of personality and all the other *balle*. I knew it all and I could shut the trap of any comrade who tried to defend Stalin. And ever

---

[37] See 'The Painter' in *The Little World of Don Camillo* (Pilot Productions, 2013) for the extraordinary story of the fanatical Gisella.

since I came back, there's never been a day at the People's Palace, in the Section or in the circle of the local group, when I don't talk about what a filthy murdering beast Stalin was. And the others have to shut up and take it, because I'm a *pioneer* of anti-Stalinism. Father, there's a whole heap of those good-for-nothings who've still got Stalin here . . . inside. They see him as a God, and I get such a kick out of seeing them suffer. I am happy now, Father, because you also know about my revenge strategy. . .'

Don Camillo was lost for words, but finally he said, 'God help you, my son. Thank you for the San Michele. I will say all the Masses you want . . . By the way, the stove in the Children's Centre is falling to bits. If you see one on your travels, let me know.'

'At your service, Father,' Ciapón assured him. 'And please, keep my story to yourself.'

After taking the canvas to a restorer in the city, Don Camillo started living in a state of frenzied agitation because the painting turned out to be a great deal more important than it had seemed at first. This meant it needed a frame to match, but beautiful frames cost a packet, and a parish priest with money is about as common as a hare with a suitcase. As for extracting money from well-to-do parishioners, his approaches were about as welcome as smoke in the eyes.

So, one morning when Ciapón appeared in front of him, and Don Camillo heard him say he had what he wanted, he stood there with his mouth open.

'What's that??'

'The stove, Father. A terracotta Becchi, clean as a whistle and good as new, not a crack in it.'

It was just what Don Camillo was looking for.

'How much are you asking for it?'

'I haven't priced it. You need to do the deal yourself. It's just around the corner, in Peppone's attic.'

Don Camillo lifted his arms to the sky.

'You're off your head! I wouldn't touch it if it was solid gold.'

'But, Father, you've got to go and see it, quick! They say you've got a camera with a flash. Bring it over. Not for the stove. The thing to photograph is in the little attic room where they kept pigeons before the war. This isn't actually the key to it, but it will open the door.'

Ciapón put a big key on the table and made to go, but Don Camillo grabbed him and the little man was forced to explain what he'd been up to.

*

Fifteen minutes later, Peppone's wife, hearing a knock at the door, went to open it and found Don Camillo on the doorstep. 'If you've come to join the Party, Father, you'll have to come back later. My husband's out.'

'This isn't politics,' replied Don Camillo, 'it's business. I heard you have a stove for sale. It might be what I'm looking for. May I see it?'

The woman grumbled something and then moved towards the stairs. It was obvious she didn't have the slightest inclination to get her hair messy with spiders' webs in the attic.

'Don't trouble yourself,' said Don Camillo. 'I can go up on my own. Assuming you'll trust me, of course . . .'

'I don't trust you . . . but the stairs are a trial,' answered the woman gracelessly.

Don Camillo went up without reply.

As soon as he was in the loft, he saw that the stove was indeed just what he needed, but he didn't waste time looking at it. What now commandeered his interest was the little room that used to house pigeons. He found the door straightaway and opened it without difficulty. He wasn't disappointed: Ciapón's description had been meticulous. The room, freshly painted, was very clean and in perfect order, and Don Camillo, who had brought his camera, started snapping away.

He was taking the last shot on his roll of film when he heard a heavy tread approaching up the stairs. He had just enough time to hide the camera under his cloak, but no time to get out of the room, and he didn't even try because it was important that Peppone should find him there.

'I wonder what Signor Archpriest would do if I reported him for trespass?'

For all his show of mockery, Peppone's voice could not conceal his profound agitation.

'I'd laugh,' replied Don Camillo. 'The Signor Mayor's good lady gave me permission to come up and look at a stove. I was simply trying to find it.'

The stove was one of those two-metre high ones with drawers, and stood directly in front of the door into the attic, so even a blind man could have found it since he'd have banged his nose on it. Don Camillo's explanation was a shameless lie.

'So, having been unable to find the stove in the attic, the reverend priest thought it would be fine to break into this private room,' sneered Peppone with distaste.

'I've not broken in to anywhere. The key was in the lock. All I did was turn it.'

Peppone took the key out of the lock and looked at it:

'Well, I should never have doubted it. No self-respecting priest goes anywhere without a bunch of dodgy keys in his pocket.'

'It seems to me that the Signor Mayor exaggerates!' exclaimed Don Camillo. 'And in any case, I haven't touched anything. I simply walked into this . . . pigeon loft-cum-sacred shrine.'

'What *shrine*!' yelled Peppone.

'The Signor Mayor's little secret.'

'It's no damned shrine!' yelled Peppone.

'Well, what would you call a clandestine room like this one, with its walls covered with grandly framed pictures of Napoleon, Garibaldi, Victor Emanuel II and Queen Helen, Girardengo,[38] Lindberg, Mussolini and Stalin? . . . A very strange shrine, Comrade Mayor. Here, for example . . . how did you come to choose an American airman flying a tin-pot little plane when you have all those glorious Soviet cosmonauts available to you?'

'Father, it is easy to go to the moon when you've got enormous power behind you like the Soviets. Lindberg crossed the Atlantic in his tin-pot plane all by himself. A man like that makes you forget that he's American.'

Don Camillo pressed on. 'And what about *him*? Why do you keep Stalin in your house when the leader of the Soviet Union and world communism has judged him to be such a villain that he's kicked his corpse out of its tomb!'

'He hasn't kicked him out of his place in history. And besides, haven't you thrown out some of your own major figures, like San Giorgio? If Saints can get purged, then why not communists?'

'May I see the stove?' enquired Don Camillo, leaving the mayoral sanctum.

'There it is,' replied Peppone, pointing to it.

'Fine,' said Don Camillo, 'send it to me at the Children's Centre in a good strong truck.'

Peppone enquired if, by any chance, Don Camillo had lost his mind. And Don Camillo explained that if he were

---

[38] A cycling champion.

not to publish a detailed photographic survey entitled *'The Comrade Mayor's secret inner sanctum'*, he would need something in return.

Put like that, the thing became a normal business transaction, and Peppone accepted the offer.

After which, Don Camillo gave the crucified Christ above the high altar a meticulously detailed account of the matter, concluding, 'Lord, how infinite indeed are the ways of Divine Providence!'

'Don Camillo,' answered Christ gently, 'why are you trying to involve Divine Providence in your reprehensible transactions?'

Don Camillo did not respond by saying that, in his opinion, supplying the Children's Centre with heating could not be called a reprehensible transaction. He thought it though.

Humour That Finds an Eternal Mark

DON CAMILLO SERIES, BOOK 1

The Little World of Don Camillo
by Giovanni Guareschi

Set in an isolated village in northern Italy, where every day eternal forces grapple with the absurd drama of life, the Don Camillo stories have been enjoyed by more than twenty-three million people worldwide. In this brand new authorised translation many stories never before translated into English are published for the first time.

In films, on television and on radio, and most recently as audiobook, Guareschi's message holds as good today as it always did, namely that what works at the level of the Little World can be made to work universally, the world over.

'Inimitable, delicious, full of pure fun.' *The Observer*

'Charming and enchanting ... Witty and wise.' *Edinburgh Evening News*

DON CAMILLO SERIES, BOOK 2

Don Camillo and His Flock
by Giovanni Guareschi

Reading the second in the Don Camillo series is to travel to the Valley of the River Po, Italy's widest and most fertile plain, with its unique atmosphere, culture and natural history. And to do so in the incomparable company of a cast of characters who testify to the exquisite humour and humanity of their creator.

'Enchanting. Hilariously funny. Strangely moving.' *BBC Radio Four*

DON CAMILLO SERIES, BOOK 3

Don Camillo and Peppone
by Giovanni Guareschi

More timeless, bittersweet stories of life in Italy's Lower Plain, more than half of which appear in English for the first time. They begin, as the last collection ended, with Don Camillo in exile in the mountains. But it isn't long before problems in the little world (in the shape of Peppone) bring him back to the presbytery door.

'The innumerable friends of *The Little World of Don Camillo* will give thanks that this Italian priest is back with us.' *The Observer*

DON CAMILLO SERIES, BOOK 4

Comrade Don Camillo
by Giovanni Guareschi

Don Camillo, as timely as he is timeless, enters enemy territory with Peppone and a group of Italian communists. The result is as much of a fiasco, and as insightful, as readers have come to expect. 'I have written this story for the "amusement" and (forgive my heavy-handedness) for the "spiritual profit" of the few friends I have left in the disjointed world of today,' wrote the author in 1963, still bitter about his treatment at the hands of his countrymen. Uniquely in the Guareschi canon, these tales, although originally published in instalments in the last fourteen issues of *Candido*, which played so important a part in the defeat of the Communist ticket in Italy, are written in such a way as to take shape as a novel.